In The Shadows

R.L. Nelson

Randee Nelson

Cover design by: Randee L Nelson; Wolf Outline by Randee L Nelson; Forest by Randee L Nelson

ISBN-13: 978-1-7356127-1-3

First Printing, 2020

For My Grandmother Mary,
You read every story that I ever wrote,
and always begged me to finish them.
I finished this one for you.
I wish you were here to read it.

Contents

IN THE SHADOWS

1

All I Wanted

"I wanted to kill someone." I take a deep breath, "I wanted to kill someone, I wanted to scream, and I wanted to run as far away as I possibly could."

"Why?" Dr. Foster asks.

"Because, after everything, she still died. She fought so hard for so long, and for what? To die alone in the middle of the night. Dad wasn't even there for her; he didn't find her until hours later when he got home from the bar." I take another deep breath; I am getting too upset. "When my mom first got sick, she said she'd always be here. It could be a stray dog or the sound of the wind, but it would be her. She'd always be there to protect us, you know?"

"But?" Dr. Foster sips his coffee.

"But the night she died, I couldn't protect her." I look anywhere but at Dr. Foster. I can't believe I admitted that.

"Smart girl." He says.

"If I'm so smart, then why haven't I gotten most of my memories back yet?" I ask.

"Okay. Here is what I think. We survive by remembering, but sometimes we survive by forgetting. You lost your mother at a young age, your brother ran away, and your father is an alcoholic. Maybe it's not such a bad thing to forget. You will figure it out, or you won't. That's how it all works." Dr. Foster takes another sip of his coffee, "It's a process, Rose. What has it been now? Six years? And you are almost finished, but you're not going to get there in a place like this."

"Wait, do you think I'm ready to stop?"

"What else do you want from me? Go home, finish school, fall in love. Live your life." He smiles and gestures for the door. "However, I expect you to call if you find that you need someone to talk to."

I stand in the hallway and stare at the wall for a few minutes, processing everything. I've been going to therapy for the last six years of my life. The doctors called it Dissociative Amnesia. A type of amnesia that happens because of a stressful or traumatic event. I would most likely regain my memories, but they didn't say for sure. They didn't say *when*. I don't even know what caused it. The only thing I *do* know is that my parents found me unconscious on the outskirts of the forest. I've been going to therapy ever since, trying to get my memories back.

Does Dr. Foster think that I won't recover? That I won't get any more of my memories back?

There is a bulletin board in front of me. Pictures of the doctors and their families cover it entirely. A postcard sticks out to me. It's one of those cheesy tourist postcards that reads:

Welcome to Paradise! Adventure where we live!

I was born and raised in Paradise. It's a small mountain town in Arizona, where most of the shops are locally owned, aside from the few corporate-owned businesses that almost every small town has. Most people think Arizona is a giant desert, though Paradise is anything but. We've got small-town charm, fourth of July fireworks, and a Christmas light parade every year. If I was older, I might be able to appreciate the things our town has to offer. To me, Paradise is a town full of nothing. The only entertainment for high schoolers here that isn't partying in the woods, is the movie theater and bowling alley.

"Rosey!" Andrew smiles, getting up from one of the plush chairs in the waiting room. Andrew Palmer is my best friend; he has been since we were kids. Or at least that's what I've been told. There is nothing romantic between us, but he is probably one of the most handsome men I've seen. His long, dark hair is up in a man-bun, revealing his brown eyes, and when he stands, he is at least a foot taller than my five-foot four-inch stature. His handsome looks make up for his lack of fashion sense; Andrew would not know how to dress even if the outfit was picked out for him. The only time I've ever even seen him matching is when we have a school dance, and he wears the same blue suit that he's had since middle school; since he reached six foot in seventh grade, he's never had to buy new clothes from growing out of them.

"Ready, player one? "He laughs, and I roll my eyes. He's also a bit of a nerd.

Deme sits on the couch, flipping through the channels on tv when I finally get home. Deme is my little sister and the exact opposite of myself. Her auburn hair is kept short around her shoulders in a bob. She is olive-skinned, short, and model skinny. She gets it from our mother. Sometimes, I find myself doing a double-take when I see her from behind.

"Did you do your homework?" I ask her, setting my bag on the floor behind the couch.

"Didn't have any," she mutters as she scrolls absentmindedly through her phone.

"Well, did you eat?" I ask.

"I was waiting for you." She tells me. I sigh and start towards the kitchen.

This is how our lives have been since mom died. I cook, clean, and work while Deme stays home. In her defense, I did tell her that she should focus on school instead of getting a job. But I can't help but feel like, if our dad stopped drinking, then things would get better around here.

He wasn't always a drinker; as kids, the only times we ever saw him drink were on holidays or at social gatherings—and even then, it was only ever a beer or two. It wasn't until Mom was diagnosed with cancer that it started to get worse. Sometimes, it was like they were both sick. As mom's cancer grew worse, so did dad's drinking. By the time she died, he was already a full-blown alcoholic. It's gotten so bad that, most nights, he doesn't even come home anymore.

I make spaghetti while Deme catches up with the Kardashians. I don't mind cooking dinner every night, and spaghetti isn't hard to make, even if you make it from scratch. I'd learned pretty quickly how to make most meals after our mom died, the biggest issue I had was not being tall enough to use the stovetop; but now that I'm sixteen and over five feet tall, it isn't an issue.

Silverware scraping the ceramic plates fills the air around us, neither of us talks. At least not until Deme has gotten halfway through her pasta.

"Thank you," she smiles before taking a sip of her water, "I didn't eat today."

"Why didn't you eat at school?" I put my fork down and try to make eye contact with her, but she avoids me.

"Oh, we had an extra cheer practice during lunch to prepare for the big game next week." she twirls her noodles around her fork before stuffing the pasta ball into her mouth.

"That's not okay, do you want me to pack you a lunch for tomorrow, so you have something in case?"

"No, I'll figure something out." she smiles, "I could always have Wyatt pick me something up when he goes off-campus for lunch tomorrow." Wyatt is Deme's boyfriend and the star quarterback of the football team at our high school. He's also a senior, which would worry me more since Deme is only a freshman, but thankfully, he's a decent guy.

After finishing her dinner, I send Deme upstairs for bed and load the dishwasher before heading to bed myself. I make sure to hit every light switch as I follow her up. I only make it halfway when a hard knock on the door stops me, and I'm forced to turn back.

"Good evening, Rose." I'm face to face with Sheriff Keller as I open the door, "I apologize if I woke you. But it seems your father was too intoxicated to drive home." Somewhere behind him, I can hear a car door opening and someone talking.

"Oh no, don't worry about it. I'd rather have him home safe than driving in his condition." I attempt to smile, but I can tell the Sheriff doesn't believe me.

"Listen, kid." He looks behind him at my dad, who's still stumbling out of the police cruiser before adding, "Is everything all right here?" My heart drops down to my stomach. The Sheriff always felt sorry for us, he was here the night that my mom died and made sure that we knew to call him if we ever needed anything, but I knew that telling him the truth would only get Deme and I placed into a group home; I have no choice but to lie straight to his face.

"Oh, of course!" I smile with more confidence than I had before, "Dad had a long day at work, and I told him not to worry about us girls for the night, that's all." I laugh, hoping that he believes me, but I don't get the chance to figure out what he is going to say, because my Dad is now stumbling up the stairs of the porch and making his way into the house. Instead of saying anything, the Sheriff smiles, tips his hat, and walks back to his cruiser. I sigh in relief, closing the door behind me.

"You know better than to answer the door on the first knock," Dad says as he stumbles over his own feet in the hallway. "And you shouldn't lie to the police, Rose." he sneers, barely able to keep his balance.

"Like you've ever given me another choice," I grumble while locking the door.

"And what," He burps, and the room is filled with the smell of rotten tacos, "Is that supposed to mean, young lady?"

"It means that if instead, I told him that, 'no, everything is not all right because our dad hasn't been home in four days and is too drunk to support his children ninety-nine percent of the time.' He would've thrown you in jail for child neglect, and Deme and I would be put in the first foster home they could find, and we'd probably never see each other again. Is that what you want, Dad? How's that for the truth?" I didn't mean to snap at him, and the words are spilling out of my mouth before I even get the chance to process what I'm going to say, but it feels good to actually get it all off my chest. Instead of answering me, however, Dad walks to the kitchen, where I hear him pop the top of a beer bottle and sit down at the table. I decide against following him and head upstairs, leaving him alone to drink away his worries.

I wake up to the sun beating down on me through the window in my room and pull the blankets over my head. I peek out only to look at my phone screen for the time and sigh; this is the fourth time this week that I've woken up before my alarm went off.

"Good morning," I jolt up, surprised to find Deme standing over me.

"Is everything okay?" I question through a yawn, and she laughs.

"Yeah, I wanted to make sure that you were up in time for breakfast." She says. I raise an eyebrow; Deme has never cooked breakfast—let alone anything besides cereal— in her life. I go to the window to look for dad's truck, but it's not in the driveway.

"Dad's not home if that's what you're looking for." Deme says, "He left early this morning."

"Of course he did." I stretch my arms out and look back at Deme, "I'll be down in a minute."

"Okay!" She says excitedly, bouncing out of my room and out of sight into the hallway. I sit back down on my bed taking in the sounds of the early morning. Birds chirp in the distance, and the neighbor's kids are screaming because they don't want to go to school. Everything is so surreal at this moment, and I can't help but feel sorry for myself. I should be like those kids, Deme should be like those kids, hell—Phoenix should've been like those kids. But, in the blink of an eye, our lives changed, and all of us had to say goodbye to our childhood. I feel guilty that mom isn't here to see the way that we have grown up to be such strong, independent people. If she were still here, maybe we would have been like those kids next door. Dad wouldn't be an alcoholic, she would still be alive, and Phoenix wouldn't have run away.

I get dressed quickly, throw my blonde hair up into a ponytail, and put a small amount of makeup on before I head downstairs. I pause at Phoenix's bedroom door. We weren't allowed to go in after he ran away because Dad didn't want us to ruin anything in case he came back, but as time went on and Nix didn't come home, Dad stopped caring. Eventually, his room became a reminder of all the horrible things that had happened when mom died, and we never talked about him again.

Deme is waiting for me in the kitchen but has already finished eating by the time I sit down. We haven't seen each other in a while, between me working and her being in cheer and having her own friends and life, Deme and I only see each other in passing. Last night was the first meal that we'd had together all week.

"How'd therapy go yesterday?" She asks as she pours coffee into her bright pink thermos that's covered in so many stickers it's hard to make any out.

"Oh! I'm done. I don't have to go back anymore."

"Wait," She turns around, spilling some coffee on the counter, "Does that mean that you remember? That you got your memories back?"

"No, Dr. Foster basically said that sitting in his office trying to remember isn't going to help anymore. At this point, the memories will either come back on their own, or they won't." I explain to her, slowly her face falls, and I can tell that she's upset that the therapy didn't help. A car honk, and Deme almost drops her thermos on the floor.

"Oh, sorry. That's Wyatt, I got to go. I'll see you later?" She says, hurriedly grabbing her bag off the floor.

"Definitely." I smile before yelling out the door behind her, "Make sure you eat today!" I hear her mumble something and the door shut.

Andrew lives a couple of streets over from me. He used to be my neighbor, but his Dad is in the military, and they were only renting at that time. They liked the area so much that they decided to move here permanently. Now his dad is stationed in California and travels back here to Arizona when he gets leave. Andrew takes drives me everywhere. He even takes me to school in the mornings, but since I woke up early, I text him saying I'll walk over to his house, and we can leave from there. I walk past a group of kids waiting for the school bus, I've only ever ridden it once or twice before, but when my parents realized that they don't have seatbelts on the buses, they started taking us to school themselves, and once Nix turned sixteen, it was his job to get us to school, I can't even remember what happened to his car when he left.

When I walk up to Andrew's house, his mom stands next to him in the driveway hugging him. His eyes meet mine; he smiles and rolls his eyes at his mom. Blair is one of the nicest women I've ever met, she's tall, with bright red hair. She's also Scottish, with skin whiter than Snow White herself. The only feature she gave to Andrew are her freckles; both are covered. Other than that, Andrew is the spitting image of his father, who is Jamaican American.

"Mom, I'll be alright." He says as he gently pulls away from her.

"Promise me that you'll call if you need anything. Okay?" She says and notices me walking up the driveway. "Rose!" She smiles and pulls me into a tight hug. Ever since my mom died, she stepped into being my mother figure. She used to bring over dinner for my sister and me for a couple of months after our mom died. Even now, she'll leave the occasional box of "leftovers" on our front porch. I know that she buys extra food for us, but I'll never tell her that.

"Morning, Mrs. Palmer, are you going somewhere?" I ask as she lets go of me.

"Oh, to see Andrew's father for a week or so." She smiles, gesturing to Andrew to put her luggage into her car.

"That's so nice. You deserve to get away for a few days," I say politely, but she still puts a stern look on her face.

"Yes, but that doesn't mean that you two can do whatever you want while I'm gone. No wild house parties, or mean old Ms. Jenkins will phone me faster than you can say grounded." She throws a look at Andrew.

"Don't worry, Andrew wouldn't know how to throw a party even if he wanted to," I tell her.

"Alright, alright, alright, we got to get to school now, Ma, I'll see you in a week." Andrew ushers her to her car. With one final wave, she's pulling out of the driveway as Andrew gets into his little red Dodge Dakota.

High school isn't a particularly important place, at least to me it isn't. Everyone seems to think it's a big deal, that what you do in these four years is going to matter in the world. Not here, not in Paradise. Paradise High School is a public school, dominated by the jocks, and the football program. Most of the other programs in the school are lacking funding, and the teachers are spending their own money to keep them afloat. But that's what happens when the only thing that the entire town is concerned with is "image," and they'd rather have a championship-winning sports team than an award-winning arts program. Like I said, High School isn't a particularly important place. Everyone else will tell you otherwise, maybe even Andrew would say that it's great. But once we're out of here and into the real world, no one will think that anymore. Most will only think of it fondly after they've had a few beers. This is why, while I'm here, I've refused to join any extracurricular classes. It's not like I'm going to college anyway, even with my four-point-zero grade point average. The only thing I'm focused on is graduating and taking care of Deme. After that, it doesn't matter what I do.

The parking lot of Paradise High School is nearly full, there used to be two lots that we could park in, but they thought it would be easier to keep an eye on the students if they all parked in the same lot. Everyone hangs out here before class too—well maybe not everyone, but mostly everyone—so if you're trying to avoid someone, chances are that you'll run into them at least three times a day. Andrew quickly pulls into a spot near the entrance building. If you're too slow to park, another student will take your spot, and you'll be forced to park down the street and walk to the high school from there, which is an extra mile away, and Andrew and I both start our day in English, which is located on the other side of the school. If we hadn't gotten a parking spot, we would've been late.

We sit through twenty minutes of morning announcements before our teacher, Mr. Daniels, addresses the class.

"Alright, who can tell me who Sisyphus is?" He asks, no one raises their hand, and he sighs before turning to the whiteboard to write everything down. "Sisyphus was the Greek king of Ephyra, which today is known as?" He turns around to face the class, and once again, no one raises their hand. He's about to call one of us randomly when he's interrupted by the classroom door opening. Mr. Daniels spins to face whatever kid has decided to come to class late, ready to give out a detention. Instead, he finds the Principal, who has a student trailing behind him that I've never seen before.

"Stephen, this is Areon Lux." He gestures to the kid behind him, "He transferred here from—" He pauses, looking at the new student again, "Where are you from again?"

"Washington," Areon states flatly, handing Mr. Daniels a piece of paper that most likely has his class schedule on it. "Right." Principal Thomas turns back to Mr. Daniels. "I'd like one of your students to show him around until he is used to our school." He turns around, faces Areon, pats him on the shoulder, and, with the fakest smile I've ever seen, says, "Welcome to the home of the Longhorns!" And walks out.

Mr. Daniels observes the paper Areon handed him and looks around the classroom, "Areon, meet Andrew. He'll be showing you around today. You can sit in that empty seat there behind him." Areon salutes Mr. Daniels and sinks down into the seat behind Andrew, with Mr. Daniels trailing behind him. Mr. Daniels slaps the paper down on Andrew's desk, making him jump in his seat a little before turning back to the whiteboard "Now, where was I? Oh yes, can anyone tell me what Ephyra is known as today?" He asks again, I look around, and once again, no one is raising their hand. "No, one? Alright, new kid, can you tell me?"

"Corinth," he answers as flatly as he had when he spoke to the principal a moment ago.

"Good try. Oh wait," Mr. Daniels' face contorts from annoyed to surprised, "Correct! Now, can anyone tell me what happened to Sisyphus?" He asks, and Areon raises his hand, "Yes, Areon?"

"Sisyphus was a cruel King and is punished for his deceitfulness and for thinking he was smarter than Zeus. His punishment is to roll a boulder up a hill, only for it to fall back down for eternity." Mr. Daniels writes his answer on the board and then turns to face the class.

"Okay, since Areon is the only one who seems to know anything. Open your textbooks and turn to page three-hundred-ninety-four and read the next chapter. I want a one-page summary of what you read, and there may or may not be a quiz on Monday on what you've read."

Andrew and I only have three classes together out of the six classes that we take, and that's only if you include lunch as a class. So, after our second period, we split up for the day until we meet back up for lunch. We could go off campus for lunch since we are sophomores, but neither of us likes spending the extra money on it. When I finally catch up with him in the lunch line, he's alone.

"Weren't you supposed to be showing the new kid around to-day?" I ask, reaching for an apple.

"He told me he had somewhere else to be," Andrew shrugs, "Maybe he went off campus." He shakes his head at the lunch lady who is offering him some salad, and I take it instead.

"Well, you should've gone with him. It's easy to get lost at this school." I say, giving him a pointed look, and he stops the line to look me dead in the eye.

"I'm not his babysitter." He spits, and I take a step back.

"Woah, okay. Who pissed in your cheerios today" I ask sarcastically, skip him in the line, and grab a side of fries.

"I don't think he likes me very much; he talks to me like I'm stupid or something," Andrew finally admits, and I pat him on the shoulder.

"He probably doesn't like it here yet; it's been two periods, and people were already whispering about him like he was some outcast," I reassure him.

"Yeah, maybe." He smiles, reaching out for a hamburger and two pudding cups.

"You should try to eat healthier," I say, although I can't fight him on it too much, the amount of coffee I drink has surely shortened my lifespan by about ten years.

"Yeah, and you should learn to live a little." He laughs.

"You call it living, I call it diabetes by age twenty-three" I smile and punch him in the shoulder. I sit down at our usual table while Andrew tries to convince the lunch lady to give him an extra basket of fries. I look around and notice Areon sitting by himself in the corner of the cafeteria. I can tell he doesn't feel like he fits in. It is the same look I had when I looked in the mirror after I lost my memory.

"Guard my food," I say to Andrew as he shovels his own into his mouth. He nods in response as I head over to where Areon is sitting. I'm about to tap his shoulder to get his attention when he's suddenly facing me, looking intently into my eyes. He has a chiseled face, like one of the Greek Gods we're studying in English. Behind his black hair, his blue eyes shine like I'm looking at the sky from inside of a bleak house.

"Are you going to say something, or are you going to stand there and stare at me all day?" He asks, pulling me out of whatever trance I was in. How long have I been staring at him? Heat rises in my cheeks.

"Sorry," I mutter, "I wanted to ask you if you wanted to sit with us."

"Us?" He repeats.

"Oh yeah, Andrew and I." I point towards where Andrew is sitting.

Areon almost snorts, "No, thanks." He states flatly, and I can feel my face getting red.

"Oh, alright. Excuse me for trying to be friendly" I roll my eyes, trying to hide my embarrassment and turn to walk away when I hear him sigh loudly.

"Wait, I'm sorry. Yeah, I'll come sit with you guys." I wait for him to gather his things before leading him back to the table Andrew and I had claimed.

"I'm Rose, by the way. Nice to meet you." I smile politely.

Areon nods in acknowledgment, "You too."

"Sup?" Andrew says monotonously. I shoot daggers at him with my eyes to get him to be nicer.

"So, where'd you move here from again?" I question, attempting to clear the awkward air that's hanging between the three of us.

"Washington," Areon says flatly, this isn't going to be quite easy.

"Where in Washington?" I try to question him further, eating a few fries.

"Have you ever been there?" His eyes meet mine; it feels like they are staring straight into my soul.

"N... No." I stutter, looking down at the table.

"Then, it doesn't matter." He says. It's the most awkward lunch that I have ever sat through. Andrew and Areon small talk a bit, but I don't say another word. The feeling I got when Areon looked at me made me feel too uneasy to focus on the conversation.

Only a handful of students are lucky enough to get a half-day schedule at our school, and when I say lucky, I mean they work really hard and pass all their classes early, so we don't need to take them again; I took extra classes my freshman year so I could have a half-day schedule the next few years. Andrew also has a half-day schedule, so I usually meet up with him at his truck after the bell for fifth hour rings. Today he's running late or something because when I get to his truck, he's not there. I spot Areon across the parking lot as he's getting into a white Jeep. After how much he knew about Greek mythology in English, it's no surprise to me that he has a half-day too. I want to go over to him to ask him what his problem is and why he was so rude at lunch, but I still can't shake off the uneasiness I felt.

"Rosey! How was your day?" Andrew shouts from out of nowhere, making me jump.

"Not over yet." I groan as he throws his bag into the truck bed and unlocks the vehicle. "So, there's this party tomorrow night." He starts the engine, not making eye contact with me.

"Party?" I look at him sideways. Andrew and I don't go to parties. Watching my father drink is as close to alcohol as I ever want to get.

"Yeah, Craig is throwing a party after the football game on Saturday, and he invited the whole school." He's trying to play it cool, which coming from Andrew isn't very.

"And you want to go because?" I ask.

"Well..." He pauses and clears his throat, "Gabby's going to be there."

"Gotcha," I smile.

"Yeah, she invited me during biology, but I didn't know how to respond. I told her maybe." He blushes.

"Oh," I laugh "So you're thinking that a little liquid courage is going to make it easier for you to talk to her."

"Yes. Yes, I do." He says.

"So then why do I have to go?" I ask, even though I already know the answer.

"I need you there for backup, in case I chicken out and need someone to talk me out of leaving early." I can't help but laugh at him.

"If you promise to get me home so I can take a nap before work, then Saturday night, I'll be the wingman of your dreams," I say.

I am immediately overwhelmed by the odor of coffee beans when I walk into work. I work at a small coffee shop called Common Grounds. It is one of the only locally-owned coffee shops left in Paradise, all of the others have closed down, most likely from lack of business. We get a decent number of customers, though. A lot of them are college students and locals who prefer our blends over the corporate ones. I throw my bag in the backroom and immediately get to work on the line of people standing behind the counter.

When it finally starts to slow down, the building is mostly empty. The only customers left are the few kids that always use the free WIFI to do their homework, and sip on the same coffee for hours. Given this free time, I head into the back, pick my bag up off the floor and hang it in my locker, when I hear the door chime. I take a deep breath and walk out of the back with the biggest smile I can muster up and then completely lose it when I see Areon standing on the other side of the counter.

"Welcome to Common Grounds, what can I make you?" I manage to squeak out.

"Are you stalking me?" Areon asks sternly. I can't tell if he's joking or not.

"Um, no. I work here?" I point at the name tag stuck onto my apron.

"I'm kidding," He rolls his eyes, "I'll take a long black." He orders.

"Coming right up." I'm nervous, and I can feel Areon's eyes on me even with my back turned to him. Normally, I am used to this, but I can't help but feel like he's overly judging me. Thankfully, Jessica walks up to the counter and finishes ringing him up, so I can focus on making his coffee.

Jessica and I used to be friends. Before my memory wipe, we were apparently really close, but when I didn't remember her, she turned to the popular crowd. A group of kids whose great-grand-somethings founded the town. There are a few exceptions to their group, of course, Jessica being one of them, and another girl, Gabby—who Andrew has the biggest crush on—is another.

"Are you new around here? I've never seen you around." Jessica asks, flipping her red hair back behind her shoulder.

"Yeah, just moved here," Areon says with the same flat tone he had been using all day, somehow though, I know Jessica isn't going to take the hint.

"Where'd you move from?" Her voice has gone at least two octaves higher.

"Washington." Man am I tired of hearing him say that.

"And what on earth made you want to move to a small town like this?" She says in her best country accent as she leans over the counter at him, undoubtedly flaunting her "assets."

"Can I get my coffee?" He says with a more panicked tone, and I can't help but laugh at the thought of Jessica making him uncomfortable. Jessica shoots daggers at me with her eyes and quickly goes back to ringing him up, handing him his change as I set the steaming hot cup of coffee down.

"Thank you." He sighs with relief and throws a couple of dollars into the tip jar before walking to one of the empty tables. Jessica motions for me to follow her into the back, I follow her.

Once we're out of earshot of all the customers, she relaxes against one of the counters. "Okay, he is so hot!" She basically shouts for the whole shop to hear, "Do you know who that is?" She asks, taking a step closer to me.

"His name is Areon, he moved here, he's in our grade. What else do you want from me?" I start pulling out bags of coffee beans and reorganize them, so it looks like I'm busy on camera. Our boss likes to watch the security cameras when he isn't here so he can make sure that we're working, and I've already been called and yelled at for Jessica not working three times this month.

"Do you think he's single?" She asks, leaning against a pile of bags I was about to move.

"Probably, he did move here from like three states away, Jess." I gently push her to the side, and she rolls her eyes at me.

"Well yeah, but that doesn't mean he doesn't have a girlfriend from back—" She stops and looks down for a minute, "Shit, where was he from again?"

"Washington and watch your language." I roll my eyes and start grabbing the coffee creamers. "Oh, right. Anyway, do you think he'd want to come to Craig's party with me?"

"You'd have to ask him, but he doesn't strike me as the party type. Or even the dating type, so good luck." I grab a bag of coffee beans and motion for her to grab the bottles of creamer before heading back out to the front counter while she follows behind me. She sets everything down onto the counter next to me and walks over to the register to grab a pen and a pad of paper. I watch her scribble something down as I refill the coffee bean canister. Jessica then stands up straight, takes a deep breath, and walks over to where Areon is sitting in the lobby. He is completely immersed in his laptop and looks annoyed as she approaches him; I have a pit in my stomach for her. Her eyes flutter as she hands—what I assume to be her phone number—to Areon. He takes it, looks it over a few times, and then nods at her. When she walks back, Jessica's face is redder than I have ever seen it before.

"How'd it go?" I ask, genuinely curious.

"It doesn't matter what he said, Rose. He'll come." She smirks. There's the smug Jessica that I know and love.

"And how do you know that?" I humor her.

"Because no man can resist looks like these. Duh." She states, gesturing at her breasts.

"Yeah, keep telling yourself that," I mumble to myself, turning back to restock for tonight.

Every Friday night is 'Open Mic Night.' Typically, this means that Friday nights are slower than normal because everyone is either out partying or at whatever sport is having a home game, but because Craig's party isn't until tomorrow night and the football game is away, the place is packed. Andrew comes in every Friday night, and normally, we'd sit in the corner and judge everyone that performed, but since there's standing room only, I have to stay near the counter. I send Andrew over to sit next to Areon; mostly because I figure Areon would hate the performers as much as we do, but also to keep Jessica away from Areon. I'm sure he would have rather sat alone, or even left, but I can tell Areon was thankful to have someone keep Jessica away from him.

"Why didn't you tell me," Jess whispers to me as the first act starts to introduce himself.

"Why didn't I tell you what?" I whisper back.

"That you are friends with him." She says, and I look at her, confused.

"I've been friends with Andrew for years. You know that," I tell her.

She shoots me a dirty look. "I meant that you are friends with Areon." She crosses her arms.

"What? No, we're not." I'm trying to pay attention to the balding man on stage as he tries to tell a joke, wishing she would drop her infatuation with Areon.

"Then why is Andrew sitting with him?" She raises an eyebrow and crosses her arms again, making it clear that she's not going to drop it.

"Because he had to show him around school today, they probably hit it off or something. I don't know." I explain, hoping she picks up on the annoyance in my voice.

"He's not a child, you know." Jess rolls her eyes at me.

"Excuse me?" I say a little too loud. A few customers look back at me angrily.

"Oh, nothing." She pats me on the arm before walking over to Areon's table again, so much for keeping her away from him.

After all of the acts have finished, the shop has pretty much cleared out, save for a few stragglers who are finishing their drinks. Jess has been non-stop flirting with Areon the entire night and is about to make her way back over to him when I stop her. I feel like a babysitter.

"Hey, I think I'll be okay the rest of the night, you can head home if you want." She looks back and forth between Areon and me for a moment and then finally looks at the clock.

"Yeah, okay." She heads into the back, grabbing her purse and hanging her apron up.

"See you tomorrow night!" She calls out to Areon as she walks out the door, but he doesn't even lift his head to acknowledge her. I start shutting down some machines and wipe down the counters so I can get out of work at a decent enough time when Andrew walks up to the counter.

"Did you want a ride home tonight?" He asks. I can see how tired he is and decide against it.

"I think I'll be okay. It's a beautiful night for a walk." I smile.

"Alright, I'm going to head out then. You sure you're going to be alright?"

"Yup. I can always call you if I need you to come and get me." I tell him.

"Alright, text me when you get home, so I know you're okay,"

"Will do. Drive safe!" I call out to him as he leaves.

When the only thing left to do in the shop is to mop, Areon is the only person left in the lobby.

"You don't have to go home, but you can't stay here," I smile, leaning against one of the tables.

"Did you need any help?" He asks, picking up his chair and flipping it over the table, "I don't mind."

"No, it's okay. I just have to mop, and then I'm out of here."

"Well, at least let me give you a ride home. It's the least I can do."

I look at him, puzzled. "The least you can do for what?" I asked.

He pulls a piece of paper from his pocket, "For trying to help keep this away from me." It is the paper that Jessica had given to him, in bubbly lettering it tells her name and number with the address to Craig's house for the party tomorrow night.

"Oh, right." I laugh, "Are you going to go?" I ask, handing him back the paper.

"Maybe," He shrugs, balling up the paper and stuffing it into his pocket, "So, how about that ride?" He asks. I'm not sure why the sudden attitude change towards me.

"Why not? I'll be done in a minute. Can you wait by the door while I mop?" I ask. He nods in response.

When I finish mopping, I usher him out the door, set the alarm, and lock the door behind me. We walk to a white Jeep that sits in the parking lot. He opens the passenger door for me and gives me a hand in before getting into the driver's seat. The jeep is brand new. It is so new that there are still protective stickers over the radio.

"So, where am I going?" He asks.

"One-twenty-seven, Cherry Street." I type the address into the GPS in his car.

It is a quiet ride, whatever music playing is so quiet, it's barely audible over the sound of the engine.

"Thanks for the ride," I say after a few minutes of silence. He only nods in response. I don't think I've heard him speak more than one hundred words in an hour; we must be getting close to his word limit.

Areon turns the volume up. We've been driving in silence since we left the coffee shop. I don't recognize the song, but it is beautiful. I look out the window, trying to distract myself. Areon's face reflects in the glass. He looks flawless, the way the moonlight shines down on his face makes him look like a God; it takes everything in me not to turn and face him. I take a deep breath and try to look past his reflection and out into the world outside of the window. There's nothing but trees and bushes, and I can't find a single thing to focus on to keep my attention away from him.

When we pull into my driveway, I notice Deme's light on in her room. She usually waits for me to get home before she goes to bed. She is as protective of me as I am her.

"Well, good night." I smile, grabbing my bag off the floor from under my seat, "Thanks again for the ride."

"It's no problem," Areon replies. He leans over me and pushes open my door, a cold rush of wind blows through the car.

"Have a good night, Rose." He tells me, giving me butterflies when he says my name.

"So, did you decide if you're going to the party or not?" I ask him.

"Not sure yet, you?"

"I'm Andrew's wingman," I shrug, "I guess I'll maybe see you there?"

"Yeah, see you." He waits for me to take a step back before leaning over and pulling the passenger door closed.

I wait until his taillights disappear before I go inside the house. Deme is waiting for me on the stairs with her arms crossed.

"Do you have any idea what time it is, young lady?" She asks, and I roll my eyes at her. "Who dropped you off?" She is smirking at me, and I can feel my cheeks blush.

"No one, just a friend from school," I tell her, attempting to brush past her.

Deme blocks my path, "A boyfriend?" The way she drags out the word boyfriend makes me feel like a child.

"No," I tell her, sounding harsher than I mean to.

"So, you watch all of your friends drive off into the distance before going upstairs?" She really isn't going to drop this.

"No, I..." I trail off. Fine, she wins. "His name is Areon, he just moved here, and Jess wouldn't stop hitting on him at the coffee shop, so I kind of saved him from her. He drove me home to say thanks." I explain to her. She raises an eyebrow and crosses her arms. She doesn't believe me. Still, she allows me to pass her and follows me into my room.

"Are you going to Craig's party tomorrow night?" She asks, flopping down onto my bed. A shirt flies off the edge onto the floor.

"How'd you know about that?" I ask.

"He invited the entire school." She states.

"Oh, right? Yeah, I'll be there, Andrew wants to go."

"So, can I help you pick out an outfit then? And, in return, you can tell me if Wyatt shows up?"

"Sure, why not?" I laugh, it is the least I can do. I never get dressed up, and most of my clothes are a few years old anyway. Maybe she will let me into her closet of name-brand goodies.

"Yay!" She jumps up and hugs me, "Get good beauty rest, and I will see you in the morning!" She bounces out of the room and shuts the door behind her. I fall back onto my bed, maybe this wasn't such a good idea.

I am covered in sweat; it is so hot in my room that it feels like I am going to burn alive. I flip the fan on next to my bed and pull the blankets over my face to block the sunlight. I am about to fall asleep when Deme bursts into my room, making me jolt upright.

"What's wrong?" I ask, looking around.

"Dad's home," she says. I get up to peek out the window, and sure enough, his truck is parked in the driveway.

"When?" I ask.

"Sometime last night," she is staring at the wall, "I didn't hear him pull in."

"Is he sleeping?" I step back from the window and move over to her.

"On the kitchen floor," She says. Of course he is.

I walk downstairs to the kitchen where, sure enough, dad is passed out on the floor. A bottle of whiskey clutched in his hands.

"Dad." I kick him lightly, but he doesn't move, "Dad, wake up." I kick him a little harder, He moans and rolls over; his eyes slowly blink open before he notices I am standing over him.

"Want to help your old man out?" He holds his hand out to me, but I turn away. I bring a pot of coffee to a boil and throw some eggs on the stove as he gently pulls himself into a chair.

"Where have you been?" I ask, although I already know the answer.

"Working." He grunts.

"You didn't come home last night," I tell him.

"And?" He glares at me, "They sent me a town over to go over some orders." He states.

"You couldn't leave a note? Or call?" I pour a cup of coffee and place it on the table for him.

"Nope." He sniffs at the coffee, before sipping at it, "It's not your responsibility to worry about me, but if it matters that much, I'm sorry."

I freeze in place, "What?"

"Rose, I made a lot of mistakes in my life." He starts.

"Dad, don't," I turn to face him, "I don't need your apologies, I need you to prove to me..." I pause, "I need you to prove to Deme that you're done making those mistakes; that you're going to be a dad again." As if that will ever happen. I flip the eggs onto a plate and call Deme down for breakfast. Dad silently slips out of the room and into his room, slamming the door behind him. Deme and I eat in silence.

"You wash, I'll dry?" I smile, trying to lighten the mood.

"How about you wash, and I'll dry?" She snatches the towel from the counter before I can even react.

"Fine, but just this once," I tell her.

"Do you think Dad means it?" She asks.

"I can't tell, but maybe." I put my hand on her shoulder, "don't get your hopes up, and remember that we'll always have each other."

"Hey! You're getting my shirt wet!" She yells and backs away from me, I splash her with the sink water, and she runs out of the room.

As I'm finishing up the dishes, my phone buzzes on the counter next to me—Andrew.

"Rose! You still up for tonight?" Andrew's voice booms from my phone.

"Yes, Andrew," I shift the phone to my shoulder.

"Awesome! When do you want me to pick you up?"

"I don't know, eight?" I tell him.

"Sounds good, did you want to stop anywhere to eat first?"

"Yeah, sounds like a plan."

"Alright, see you at eight!" Andrew hangs up. He never says goodbye, and as annoying as it is, I can't bring myself to say it either.

Upstairs, I cross the hall to Deme's room and sit down on her bed. She is rummaging around in her closet, throwing clothes on the floor as she digs deeper.

"You ready for the fashion show?" She asks as she turns around, at least eight outfits are draped over her arm.

"Please don't make me try on like one hundred outfits," I groan.

"Okay, fine, ninety-nine outfits it is!" She laughs. I throw one of her pillows at her, but she dodges it and drops the pile of clothes in my lap.

After almost an hour of trying on clothes, Deme finally settles on a pair of nice jeans and a yellow long sleeve shirt with a green vest.

"Now for shoes," Deme says, kneeling into the bottom of her closet.

"No way you're putting me in anything with heels," I protest.

"Fine." She grabs a pair of green Chuck Taylor's out and sets them next to me,

"Thank you," I smile. I get dressed in the bathroom and come back to her room to show her the result, to which she claps before she forces me to her vanity to do my hair and makeup.

Four soft knocks echo upstairs to my room, I text Andrew to come in and that I am upstairs. Moments later, he is leaning in the doorway.

"So, where do you want to eat?" He asks.

"Doesn't matter to me, what're you hungry for? You're the picky eater." I joke.

"I'm not picky!" He defends himself.

"Oh right, you eat everything," I laugh. I grab a shoulder bag and throw it on, "So, how do I look?"

"Like Deme," he states.

I change the subject, "Ray's diner?" I ask, knowing he won't say no. Ray's is one of the only places in town that serves breakfast all day and is open twenty-four hours.

"You're okay with breakfast?" he looks shocked.

"No, but I'd kill for one of their quesadillas." I push past him, and we head downstairs.

"Are you sure?" he asks, "We can go somewhere else."

"Yeah, I'm sure. You always want breakfast, and I don't care what we eat. So, it's perfect." I laugh, "Now, let's get out of here before your stomach yells at me again."

We aren't the only group of teenagers who thought to eat before the party. When we finally walk inside the building, the place is packed with our classmates.

"So, what time is everyone going to be there?" I ask as we sit in a corner booth.

"Not sure, probably around nine," Andrew says, picking up one of the menus and flipping through it. A middle-aged woman walks towards our booth. She has the same red hair as Jessica, and I wonder if they are related.

"What can I start you off with to drink?" she asks, not looking up from her pad of paper.

"I'll have a water," I say as nicely as possible, and Andrew says the same.

"Do you think Jess is related to her?" I ask Andrew when the waitress is out of earshot.

"Her?" he asks, looking up from his menu to make eye contact before looking back down at it.

"Our waitress," I clarify, skimming over the menu in front of me.

"Don't know, ask her the next time you work together. Do you think the food is fresh or pre-made?" Andrew questions not even bothering to look up.

"Why don't you ask her?" I tell him as our waitress arrives with our drinks.

"Y'all ready to order?" She asks as she sets down the glasses of water. Andrew orders a sandwich that is stuffed with mozzarella sticks. I go with my gut and order a cheese quesadilla with a side of Pico-De-Gallo and sour cream.

"So, Gabby?" I ask, trying to hide my smile as I thumb through Instagram on my phone.

"What about her?" Andrew looks up at me, clearly nervous.

"What do you mean? What about her? What do you think is going to happen tonight with her?" I set my phone down on the table and cross my arms, "Come on, you can tell me."

Andrew blushes, "She's... She's great. She's funny and beautiful. I don't know, it's hard to describe. But I'm not going to try anything with her tonight if that's what you're asking. I don't want to, not on the first night, at least." Andrew goes on talking about Gabby, while I get lost in thought about Areon. "Are you okay?" Andrew asks, pulling me out of my head, "You don't have to come tonight if you're not up to it."

"No, I'm okay. I'm one hundred percent up for it," I smile as our waitress brings our food out. I barely touch my food while Andrew devours his in one bite. Our waitress hasn't checked on us since she brought our food out, and I find myself getting increasingly irritated as we wait for her to bring us our check. I don't feel right, not only about the party but about myself either, I have a bad feeling about everything. Ray's always has the worst service, so I should be used to it by now; if it wasn't a tweaker serving us, it was usually an annoyed waitress like the one we had tonight.

Andrew waves his hand in front of my face, "Hello? Earth to Rose!"

"Sorry, I was spacing out. What's up?"

"Are you sure that you want to go tonight? I can take you home if you want." I shake my head, part of me wants to see if Areon will show up and the other half wants to make sure Andrew has a good time.

"Alright, well, since we haven't gotten the check, do you want to go upfront and pay? I'm sure they can look up our order and ring us up there." He slides out of the booth, and I follow him up to the counter. I briefly consider leaving our waitress a bad tip, but it doesn't feel right doing that, so I leave her twenty percent. Being a waitress, I know better than to tip poorly, it is something that we depend on to live, and she could've had an awful night; who am I to judge?

2

Oh God

The party has already begun as we arrive. Fifty cars are parked on the side of the road, and there are people everywhere. We make our way up to the front door and let ourselves in. No one would have heard us knock if we tried. We push past a huge group of people in the hall and find ourselves in the kitchen where we find Craig.

"Hey! You guys made it; glad you could come. The booze is out back in the barn; there are three beer kegs and about ten diverse types of Vodka and Rum." He explains as Andrew helps him lift a keg, "Oh, and please stay away from the animals, I don't need anybody falling asleep in the pigpen and getting eaten." He winks. This does little to calm my nerves.

"Good to know," I laugh nervously, and I follow them out to the back yard. Everyone cheers at the sight of another keg. It looks like the whole school is here and maybe some kids from the next town over. Craig is lucky that he lives so far out of town, and the closest neighbor lives over a mile away, or the cops would've been here in an instant.

I follow the boys into the barn, and I am amazed by how much time Craig has put into decorating. There are white Christmas lights strung throughout the banisters, a make-shift bar in the back of the barn, and Bluetooth speakers strategically placed every thirty feet or so. I head over to the bar and grab a beer for Andrew and me. Craig thanks Andrew and explains that his older sister had gotten married in the barn this past weekend before being pulled away by some other football players; I should've known Craig would never decorate for a party.

We leave the crowded barn and head for an area where a few tables have been set up for beer pong. Cheerleaders versus football players. I nudge Andrew and gesture towards a group of people sitting around a bonfire, but Andrew is already looking at it. I look closer to see what he is staring at and find it. Gabby is laughing with some of her friends around the fire.

"Go talk to her, that's the reason we're here, isn't it?" I ask, crossing my arms but being careful not to spill my beer in the process.

"Well, yeah." He looks at his beer through the firelight, "I think I need to drink more first, though." He chugs the rest of his beer, and we walk back to the barn in time for Craig to announce, 'Community Shots.' I'm sure how he got his hands on one hundred shot glasses, but figure they are another leftover from the wedding. Everyone gathers around as shots are passed out. Once they are, Craig quiets the music and everyone down.

"How's everyone doing tonight?" He asks, and everyone cheers in response, "Good! Now you're all probably wondering why I invited everyone over tonight," He pauses for a moment, "As you all know, our team is about to get to state!" The football team starts cheering, but Craig shushes them, "We're all in this together! If we're going to win, then we're going to need all of you out there cheering for the Longhorns!" Someone behind us howls, others laugh. "Now, let's all raise our glasses and toast to the Longhorns winning the State Championship!" It's the cheesiest toast anyone has ever given at a party and probably the worst too, but everyone raises their cups to each other's, and we all take a shot together. I down the clear bitter liquid and rinse my mouth with beer.

Andrew and I make our way back to the bar. I pour myself a mixed drink of Vodka and watermelon juice while Andrew grabs a beer and a shot of whiskey. I raise my eyebrow at him, but he ignores me and walks out toward the bonfire. I follow him silently through the crowd of people, and we make our way to the fire where Gabby is sitting with a few of her friends from school. We sit across from her, and she smiles when she sees him, ignoring me completely. Getting ignored makes my blood boil, the alcohol probably doesn't help either. How does my dad drink this stuff all the time? My skin feels so hot I can't stand it. Andrew is making small talk with her now; she looks drunk already. I wonder how long she's been here.

"Hey, are you okay?" Gabby asks me, finally acknowledging my existence.

"Yeah, I'm fine." I sip at my mixed drink.

"Are you sure? You don't look so good." She asks again.

"Yeah, I'm hot." I laugh. I'm not lying, we are so close to the fire, it feels like it is licking at my skin. I look up at the stars and the full moon. A slight breeze blows, and I close my eyes, basking in its coolness.

"Hey, do you think Areon is going to show up?" My eyes snap open. Jessica is now sitting next to Gabby.

"I don't know. Why do you even like him? He dresses like an emo." Gabby asks her, and Jessica rolls her eyes. I watch her as she scans the crowd looking for him before locking eyes with me.

"Rose, you seem to be buddy-buddy with him; do you think he's going to show up?"

"I'm not sure. He didn't say anything when he drove me home last night." I don't break eye contact with her, and she gives me a dirty look.

"He took you home last night?" Andrew asks, making me feel a little guilty for not telling him.

"He stayed until closing and offered to take me home," I explain, Gabby is looking at Andrew now. I can tell she likes him, but like most girls that Andrew has dated over the years, she is probably afraid that there is something going on between us. This conversation isn't helping any. I want to tell her not to worry, that there is nothing going on between Andrew and I. Somehow, I feel like it will make things worse though.

"I'm going to go see if Wyatt is here," I say, standing up. I lose my balance a bit, but Gabby grabs my hand to help me balance myself, "Thanks." I smile. I stagger towards the barn again. If anyone knew where Wyatt could be, it would be his best friend, Craig.

I find Craig inside, where he and his other football buddies are smoking something. I could smell it the second I walked in here. It was as if a skunk had sprayed the entire football team.

"Hey, Rose, are you having a good time?" Craig asks.

"Yeah, it's a great party." I smile, "Have you seen Wyatt tonight?"

He smiles back, "Nah, he didn't come. Said something about wanting to hang out with your sister instead." He winks. I ignore what he might be insinuating with his wink.

"Alright, thanks, I'll let you get back to hosting the best party of the year now," I tell him. He smiles and holds his red solo cup in the air.

"To the best party of the year!" he smashes our cups together, spilling more than half of mine onto the floor and takes a drink before getting distracted by the head cheerleader. I throw my empty cup away and head to the barn for a new one.

It's midnight, I'm drunk, and I am ready for bed, but I can't find Andrew, and there is no way I am going to be able to walk over fifteen miles to my house this late at night. There are people everywhere, dancing and drinking and laughing. There is no way that I am going to be able to search for Andrew productively. How much have I had to drink? I lost count sometime after the third round of community shots. I make my way out to the front yard for fresh air, and I see Andrew's truck a couple of cars down the road and head straight for it. I pull the tailgate down and lay on the truck bed. The breeze feels good against my skin, and the night sky is beautiful. Why didn't I think of coming out here sooner?

"Hey, Rosey, how's it going?" I sit up, expecting to see Andrew stumbling toward the truck, but it isn't him, it's one of the jocks from our school, Tyler. I don't say anything, but instead, I lay back down, ignoring him. "Oh, come on, don't leave me hanging" He laughs, I sit back up and mean-mug him. Tyler makes his way onto the edge of the truck bed and puts his arm around my waist. I shrug away from him and slide as close as I can to the edge of the truck and farther away from him, I have never hung out with him before, so I have no idea why he is being so pushy with me.

"Leave me alone, Tyler," I demand, although I don't sound so convincing. I am never drinking again.

"Come on, babe," He scoots closer to me, and I jump off the edge of the truck bed.

"I'm not your babe, and I think you should go now," He isn't having it though, his eyes fill with rage.

"Come on, don't be a tease," he says, grabbing my waist again and pulling me into him. I try pushing away from him, but even with the alcohol in his system, he is stronger than me.

"Let me go, Tyler," I warn. He ignores me, wrapping his arms around my waist. I can feel his breath on my neck, and I'm overwhelmed by the smell of alcohol.

"I know you want me." He whispers drunkenly into my ear. I shudder, trying to get out of his grasp, but I can't. Nothing I do is working, and he holds me so tight that I can barely move my arms.

"I said stop, please. Leave me alone!" I am desperate now; I feel my body shaking under his muscles as he grips me tighter. I can barely breathe. I don't have enough strength in me to fight him off, and before I know it, he is pulling me back onto the truck bed and climbing on top of me. I try screaming for help, but he grabs my throat. He holds it so tightly that no sound can escape my lips. My vision is getting spotty from the lack of oxygen, and I know that any second now, I am going to pass out, and he can do whatever he wants to me.

Why did I even come here? If it weren't for Andrew, I would have been unharmed at home, but he wanted me to come with him, and I wanted to have a good time. I can feel the anger boiling in my blood. I can't believe this is happening to me. It's my fault. I should've gone back inside the second he came over to me, but I want to blame Andrew more than anything. He is the reason I'm here, the reason I am in this mess. If it weren't for Gabby and Andrew, I wouldn't have had to leave the fire, surrounded by people to keep me safe.

My heart's beating faster than I've ever felt it beat in my entire life, my blood is boiling, and it feels like Tyler's hand is inside of my throat he's gripping it so hard, his other hand is trying to pull my pants down, but he can't figure out how; he's drunker than I thought. I can feel him filling with rage. Suddenly, he slams his fist into the bed of the truck out of anger, inches away from my head.

"Stop fighting it, I know you want me!" He yells.

"Please." I whimper, "Please stop." I'm crying now. Angry, desperate tears fall from my eyes. I can't breathe, and I can't see anything. Why isn't anyone helping me? How did nobody hear him yell? The music is too loud. I can feel it vibrating the truck. My bones feel like they are going to break under the weight of him on top of me. My back arches. It feels like my spine is popping in and out of place. I try to scream, but I can't. He still has a firm grip on my throat.

Air. I need air.

I take a deep breath. Then another. And finally, let out a sigh of relief. Tyler is no longer on top of me. I can't see him anywhere, but I take advantage of being free and feel my way around for the end of the tailgate. When I find the edge, I roll out. I was going to run, but the second I hit the ground, I feel a hand grab my arm and yank me up onto my feet. I try to run, but I can't. I begin pushing away from whoever is holding me. Praying that it isn't Tyler.

"Rose!" That isn't Tyler's voice. I look up and find myself face to face with Areon. I stop thrashing and relax into him.

"Are you okay?" He asks. I nod and attempt to say something, but Areon shushes me. "Save your strength," he bends down and grabs my legs, lifting me into the air. I don't know where he is taking me, but I don't care. I would rather be anywhere but here. My breathing slows. Tyler is gone, or at least I can't see him if he is still here. I didn't even hear Areon approach or make any sound at all. Did I pass out? Or did I just black out? I have no idea. Areon put me in the passenger seat of his jeep, and I curl into a ball against the cold leather seat. I immediately feel sore. Now that the adrenaline has left me, even the thought of moving makes my body hurt. Areon starts the car before turning to buckle my seatbelt.

"Do you want the AC on?" He asks. I nod in response.

"What...happened?" I force myself to speak, but I sound nothing like myself, and my throat is on fire.

"Don't worry, he can't hurt you anymore," Areon says, and I look up at him. Something about the way he worded that makes me feel uneasy, "He got exactly what he deserved." He pulls away from the side of the road, and I watch the white Christmas lights fade away in the side mirror. "Let's get you home." Areon places his hand on my knee, in a comforting way. But I jerk away from his touch, and he pulls away.

"I should probably let Andrew know I'm leaving and that I'll be okay." I croak. Areon slams on the breaks, I slide forward in the seat, hitting my knees on the dashboard. You'd think my body shattered against the glovebox, the way I scream.

"What?" His knuckles turn white around the steering wheel, "You seriously want to tell him you're okay? He doesn't even know what happened to you!" He yells. I feel a tear run down my cheek. I was so mad at Andrew for bringing me here moments ago. Areon is right, I shouldn't want to look at Andrew, let alone talk to him or tell him what happened to me. I can't help but want to let him know that I was at least leaving, but maybe disappearing would be better. That way, he wouldn't try to find me and take me home and would stay with Gabby or whoever he was with. Maybe I shouldn't even tell Andrew about what happened. I don't even know what happened.

"Oh my god," I whisper, "What happened to me?" I look up at Areon, my eyes fill with tears.

"Rose, you should save your voice. You're already starting to bruise." Areon tells me.

"Tyler tried to hurt me," I ignore him and look at my arms, they are covered in tiny purple spots. He is right, I shouldn't be talking right now. I can feel my throat closing, and I'm hungry for more air, but I need to hear him say something, anything, to let me know that what happened was real.

"Rose..." He starts but trails off, his gaze softens. He reaches out and entwines his finger in mine. I look down at his hand on mine for a moment. I never want him to let go. But I pull my hand away and turn to the window. Areon's reflection stares back at me through the glass.

"Rose, you didn't deserve that. Now, please, let me take you home." He pleads.

"I don't want to go home," I whisper. It's all I can do now.

"Then, where do I need to take you?" He asks. Laughing. Footsteps. In the side mirror, I can make out people walking to their cars in the distance. The dashboard reads two o'clock.

"What happened to Tyler?" I ask, looking back at the mirror. A couple of girls drunkenly make their way to their car, giggling about something.

"I told you not to worry about him," Areon says, "He's knocked out on the side of the road, someone will find him. He'll be fine." I lift my hand and reach for his, he takes it without hesitation. We lock eyes. He doesn't know what to say to me.

"You can take me home," I whisper, his hand relaxes in mine before he pulls it away. I close my eyes and rest my head on the center console, letting sleep overtake me.

I wake up in a room I don't recognize. I sit up and look around. I'm bundled in deep black blankets that smell like vanilla. I hear movement from another room, dishes clinking, and what sounds like a coffee pot being placed into a coffee maker. I have no idea where I am. I pull the blankets off me and suppress a scream. I lay back down, my head throbs, and every part of my body is bruised. I hold out my arm and poke at the deep purple and black bruises that cover it. I was attacked. Areon saved me. I am safe. Footsteps approach the door, and it opens. Areon comes in, carrying a tray.

"How do you feel?" He asks, setting the tray on the bedside table. Toast and coffee. I do my best to sit up, and Areon hands me the coffee mug.

I sip the hot coffee; it needs more sugar. "Awful," I tell him. My voice is still hoarse.

"That's expected," Areon chuckles.

"Where am I?" I attempt to look around again, but my neck muscles prevent me from moving too much.

"You're at my house. Here," He takes the coffee from my hands and gives me a piece of toast instead, "Do you remember what happened last night?"

I nod, "For the most part," I say, "Why are you being so nice to me?"

"Because, for some reason, I care about you." He says without blinking. I get butterflies in my stomach. I can't speak. "Eat," He says, taking the toast from my hands and lifting it to my mouth.

"I can feed myself," I tell him, taking the toast back.

"My sisters have some clothes you can take; their room is across the hall. I'll be in the shower if you need me." He stands and goes to the closet, digs a few things out of it, and leaves the room without looking back.

After eating, I slowly make my way across the hall to Areon's sisters' room, using the wall to support me. I browse through a few of the clothes on the hanger before I realize that I don't even know his sisters' names. I didn't even know he had sisters. I grab a T-shirt from one of the hangers and turn to the dresser to find some shorts or something. I find a pair of black workout shorts in the top drawer and strip down, only to start crying the second I look at myself. Dark bruises cover most of my skin. How am I going to hide these? I pull my hair back with the scrunchie on my wrist and hesitantly look in the mirror on the other side of the room, More bruises. There is a light knock on the door, and I open it. Areon comes and leans against the doorframe about to say something but stops when he catches sight of my neck. I pull the scrunchie out of my hair, letting it fall back down around my shoulders.

"How am I going to cover this up?" I ask him. Areon brushes the hair away from my neck and observes the bruises while tracing his fingers over them; I get goosebumps on my arms.

"You took a pretty hard fall." He says out of the blue.

"Pardon?" I observe his face, but he shows no emotion.

"At the party, I watched you fall into a ditch. You were pretty drunk, and I couldn't remember where you lived, so I brought you here." He explains.

"What are you talking about?" I must look offended because he furrows his brows.

"You asked how you were going to cover it up. I mean if you really don't want anyone to know the truth." He says.

"What about my neck?" I ask.

"You own makeup, don't you?" He raises his eyebrows, crosses his arms, and leans into the door frame; I could have melted right where I was standing. Instead, I glare at him.

"So, when do I get to go home?" I ask.

"Whenever you want. You said you didn't want to go home last night, so I brought you here." He states. I vaguely remember telling him I didn't want to go home. I don't know why I would say that, maybe I didn't want to face Deme. Oh no.

"Where's my phone?" I ask, picking up my old pants and digging in the pockets. I come up empty.

"Maybe in my car, I don't know. I'll go look for you."

"Thank you," I smile. He disappears in the hallway. I make my way through the hallways and find the kitchen. This house looks almost abandoned, there is a thick layer of dust on a lot of the furniture and the paint on the walls is peeling. Where is his family? His sisters can't be much older than him, since most of their clothes are the same brands that Deme wears. There are also no pictures of anyone on the walls. Areon walks into the kitchen and waves my phone before handing it to me. There are ten missed calls and even more unread texts. The calls are from Deme, no doubt wondering what happened and why I didn't come home last night. The texts are from a few people. I decide to read the ones from Andrew first.

They are pretty normal. He thanks me for giving him and Gabby some alone time in the first text. Progressively, the texts get sloppier, most likely due to the amounts of alcohol he had been drinking. The most recent text from him reads:

'Hey Rose, sorry about last night. I couldn't find you or get a hold of you, and Gabby really needed a ride home, so that's why I left without you. I hope you can forgive me. I'm really sorry.'

I'm annoyed. He knew that he left me behind but didn't think to tell me until this morning. I scroll through the rest of the messages, barely reading them.

"Everything alright?" Areon asks when I set my phone down on the kitchen table.

"I guess so," I pick my phone back up and send Deme a text saying I am okay and that I will be home later. She tries calling, but I send it to voicemail.

"So, what's the verdict? Home or not?" Areon asks. I look up at him. There is a scar on his eyebrow that I hadn't noticed before.

"Not yet," I reply, "Please? I don't want to jump into that yet."

"That's fine with me. Want to do anything, or do you want to sit here all day?"

"Whatever you want, it's your house, your car, your choice," I tell him.

"Alright then, get in the car, and let's go." He smiles, holding the front door open for me.

"Where are we?" I ask. We have been driving for thirty minutes to the middle of nowhere. The dense tree lines along the dirt road make me feel like we are entering a whole new world.

"Somewhere I like to come to get away from everything." He says. The dirt road ends, and we park as close to a tree as we can. "Feel up to walking?" Areon asks, and I nod. I'm not sure how fast

I'll be, but maybe getting my muscles working will be good for the pain. Before I can get my seatbelt off, Areon is already opening my door.

"Thank you," I smile, taking his hand and stepping out of the vehicle.

We walk in silence for a couple of minutes before I decide to break the ice.

"So, what made you go to the party last night?" I ask him.

"I figured I might as well try to make some friends if I'm going to be here for a while." He says, although he doesn't sound very sure of his answer. The fresh air is amazing; I can't remember the last time I spent this much time outdoors.

"So how often do you come out here?" I ask, and he walks a few feet in front of me.

"I try to come out here once a week." He looks back and slows his pace to match mine. We walk together for another mile or so until I need to stop. I rest up on a flat boulder while Areon looks onward.

"So, are we walking still, or is this it?" I ask, secretly hoping I don't have to walk anymore.

"It's a little further, are you ready?" I smile, but internally, I'm screaming. I stand up, and my knees shake. Areon chuckles to himself, and I hold back from giving him a dirty look.

I am speechless. We arrive at the edge of a cliff that overlooks the entirety of our town. Pine trees encircle us on the mountain side and run down the sides of the cliff, gradually making their way to Paradise. Only the sound of the wind surrounds us, and there are no busy sounds of traffic and everyday life. I feel more at peace than I ever have. Areon sits on the edge, dangling his feet off, I follow suit.

"It's beautiful out here. I was going to ask why you came out here, but I can see why; it's breathtaking."

"It's a good place to come to clear your head," he tells me, staring off into the distance.

"It's nice to get away from everything every once in a while." I
agree. I wish I'd known about this place sooner. Although I wouldn't
have had a way to get out here by myself and I don't see Andrew
wanting to spend the gas money to get here.

"Are you feeling okay?" he asks.

"I'm doing the best I can right now," I tell him. He doesn't say
anything else. I look out at Paradise. I can't make any people out,
but cars drive down the streets. They look like ants from here. You
can't see Craig's house from here. I'm curious if anyone is still here
at this hour. Tyler worms his way into my mind, and I can't help but
wonder what happened last night.

I lay back, not wanting to stare at our small town any longer and
rest my head on my arms. The way Tyler was on me one moment
and gone the next doesn't make sense. I must have passed out for a
few minutes. It would have been a struggle to pick Tyler off me. He
easily weighed over two hundred and fifty pounds, Areon can't be
more than one-eighty. Maybe Areon was able to pull him off me,
that would be more plausible. I want to ask Areon what really happened, but I can't get the words out of my mouth. Maybe part of
me doesn't want to know. I look up at Areon, surprised to find that
he is already watching me. Our eyes meet. Something about them
makes me feel like he can read my mind, I'm not sure what or how
he would be able to.

"I'm sorry that happened to you." He says, maybe he can read
minds.

"I'm lucky that you were there to help me," I tell him. He breaks
eye contact and stares out over the trees.

We sit silently together, neither of us breaking the beautiful silence of the world around us. Birds chirp in the distance, and the
sun sinks farther down. I can still feel every bruise on my body. A
few times, I find Areon staring at the ones on my neck. I can cover
the ones on my arms and legs with clothes easily, but the ones on

my neck are going to be a lot more difficult. In a way, I'm glad to have them. I have the proof that it really happened, that it wasn't just a dream or something. Was Areon leaving the party when he found us, or just showing up? And what am I going to tell everyone? The story that I fell is only going to go so far before people start to question it, and Deme won't believe it. Do I tell anyone the truth? Should I keep it a secret? I feel so conflicted. He was intoxicated and didn't know what he was doing. Maybe he doesn't even remember doing it. I feel a tear falls down my cheek. I've turned away from Areon, so he can't see me crying, even though he already has. I'm too late though, He wraps his hair around me and pulls my head to his chest gently. He is warm and vaguely smells like my dad's cologne. Teakwood, that's what it was called. Mom used to buy it for him every Christmas.

I'm not sure how long we stay this way, but we watch the sun go down together. Silently, the giant burning sphere sinks towards the horizon, coloring the rock layers a bright orange until it is gone, and Paradise has turned to shadow. It's late, the sun sets around six-thirty, and I should've been home by now. But I don't want to leave. Up here, it feels like my world is perfect. Even though I know it won't last, I want to soak up every second of it. Areon shifts, and I look up at him. He could kiss me. Wrap his fingers in my hair and mine in his.

"Are you ready to head back?" He asks, shattering my desire.

"Yeah, I think so," I say.

The walk back to Areon's jeep feels even longer than when we first walked out here. Areon walks ahead of me with the flashlight while I trail behind him.

"Thank you," I tell him.

"For what?" He asks, slowing his pace down so I can keep up with him.

"For today. For everything you've done for me. I appreciate it."
I push the hair from my eyes, and Areon stops to face me. I almost
bump into him.

"You deserved to have a good day after what happened to you."
He speaks with barely a whisper. His face only inches from mine, I
become aware of how awful I must look this closely. He must sense
how insecure I am because he chuckles and brushes my hair behind
my ear. I am ready for him to kiss me, but instead, he looks down
at the ground and turns to keep walking. I follow behind him again,
a little closer than before, due to the darkness growing in the sur-
rounding forest. I feel safe with him.

Back at the car, Areon gives me a hand into the passenger seat
before getting in himself.

"So, are you ready to go home yet?" he asks.

"Yeah, I think so," I say while struggling with the seatbelt, "Did
you need the address again?"

"No, I remember." He says, reaching over and clicking my seatbelt into place.

"I thought you said you didn't remember where I lived," I say.

"I did, but bringing you home at three in the morning, covered
in bruises and passed out didn't seem like a clever idea." He tells
me as we get back onto the road. He's right. If not dad, then Deme
would've been the one to answer the door, and she would freak out
if I'd had a minor cat scratch. Areon turns the radio on and flips
through a few channels before hooking his phone up to the Bluetooth. He scrolls through a few songs while keeping his eyes on the
road before stopping on a song I've never heard before. As we drive,
I can't help but wonder why Areon is being so nice to me when he is
so short with everyone else. He barely even glanced at Jess and had
already proven to want to be around anyone other than Andrew.
Why had he even gone to the party? He obviously didn't like being
with or around people, so what was the point? When I'd asked him

earlier, he made a decent excuse, but his tone made it seem like he was lying. I won't ask him again, the last thing I need is to get on his bad side for repeating the same questions to him over and over again.

We pull into my driveway; dad's truck is parked out front, and Deme's bedroom light is on. Areon turns the jeep off and walks around to my door to open it.

"Thanks again," I smile, accepting his hand to get out.

"I'll see you at school?" He asks, and I nod. I slowly make my way to the front door while listening to Areon pull out of my driveway.

Deme isn't waiting for me by the stairs like last time, but I can hear my dad fumbling around with something in the kitchen. I tip-toe my way to my room and lock the door behind me. I slump down into the chair in front of my vanity and stare at myself in the mirror; I look awful. My hair is barely covering the bruises on my neck, and I'm glad that Deme didn't meet me at the door. I bury my face in my hands and take a deep breath. I should shower. I peek out my bedroom door and sneak into the bathroom, being sure to lock the door behind me before I get undressed. I barely recognize myself. Bruises mark my body, making me look like a purple and white cheetah. I tear myself away from the mirror and start the shower, climbing into the tub. The water feels amazing on my skin. I soak in the sound of the water as it beads down on my skin and close my eyes for a moment. Tears pour down my face and mix with the warm water. Hopefully, the sound of the water muffles my cries. What almost happened to me? What would you even call it?

Nothing. Nothing happened.

Areon stopped it before anything could happen. I fell at the party. That is what I will say if people ask. I will cover the bruises on my neck with makeup and wear a scarf if I need to. No one needs to know. And no one will know.

Deme is waiting for me on the other side of the bathroom door when I got out of the shower. I panic when she knocks.

"Rose? Can I come in?" She asks lightly, her voice barely over a whisper. I wipe the mirror off, wrap myself with a towel, and rough up my hair around my neck to hide the bruises again before opening the door.

"Sorry I didn't come to see you first thing; I really needed a shower," I say, brushing past her in the doorway and making my way to my room.

"That's okay," She stares at me, studying my face. "I heard you crying." She adds. Straight to the point. Here we go. This is where the lies start.

"Oh, I'm fine," I tell her, I dig in my closet for some pajamas and try to laugh.

"Oh, yeah? Then what's this?" she pokes the back of my neck—*hard.* I wince in pain. "And what about these." She pokes at the bruises on my legs.

"What's what?" I try to play it off like I have no idea what she is talking about.

"The bruises on your body, Rose." She crosses her arms.

"Oh, that? I fell at the party the other night; it's really nothing." My eyes avoid hers; there is no way that she believes me. I wouldn't believe her if the tables were turned.

"Really? Cause it looks like someone hit you in the back of the head with a two-by-four." She states. I don't say anything. Lying to Deme is so hard. "Fine, if you don't want to talk, then I'll ask someone else," she says, storming out of my room. I haven't lied to Deme since we were kids, and it killed me to do it now, but I can't tell her the truth. Not when I don't even know what the whole truth was; I didn't even know what Areon did to Tyler. And I won't be the victim.

I stay in my room until I don't hear any noise in the house. I walk downstairs. I can hear my dad snoring behind his bedroom door, and Deme had gone to bed hours ago. I sneak into the kitchen and pull the milk out of the fridge to pour a glass, but I forgot to finish the dishes, and there are no clean cups. Typical. I used to do all the dishes when I was a kid for an allowance, and doing it now almost calms me. I'm glad to have some sort of normalcy. Coughing in my dad's room startles me, and I almost drop a plate. He grunts, and I hear his footsteps; he is probably about to get ready for work. Is it already that early in the morning? I know he gets up an hour before he has to leave, but that means that it is almost time for Deme and me to start getting ready for school. I check my phone, it's midnight. I wait for him to stop moving around, hear a toilet flush, and then nothing, so I go back to doing the dishes.

I head back upstairs after finishing the dishes and lay down on my bed. It feels good to be in my own bed, but I'm still not tired. I scroll through Facebook for a while on my phone. I hadn't been on any social media since right before the party and didn't realize that I had so many notifications waiting for me when I opened the app. My news feed is flooded with pictures from the party. Most of them are pictures of the football players and the other popular kids, but there are a few of Andrew with Gabby and even a few of me. I almost drop my phone when I find one that was taken outside by someone's car. Andrew's truck is in the background of the picture, and there are two people in the back of it. You can't tell who it is, which I am thankful for. But I know who it is, and that's enough to make my heart sink. It's Tyler and me. He has his arm around me. I can't look away from it. I study it harder than I've studied anything in my life. As I go to put my phone away, I notice something new, Areon. He's standing behind the truck watching us. I wouldn't have been able to tell it was him if I hadn't seen what he was wearing, and at first, I thought my eyes were lying to me and that I was seeing things. Even after zooming in as much as I can, I am one hundred percent sure that Areon is standing there staring at me, at us. I check who was tagged in the picture, but it was the three girls who were posing in the middle. I go to the comments next. Nothing.

This is the only bit of evidence I have as to what had happened. How long had Areon been standing there for, and why hadn't those girls noticed what Tyler was trying to do to me? My mind races with questions that I don't know the answer to, and I'm sure that the only one that can answer those questions is Areon.

3

In The Shadows

I can't sleep, and if I did, it wasn't for more than an hour. I do not want to go to school today. Every inch of my body screams in pain with every step I take. I'm not sure if I can pretend not to be so hurt. Andrew will be here in an hour, plenty of time to call and tell him not to come, but as much as I don't want to go, part of me *does* want to. I get dressed and ready, but this time, I am careful to cover the bruises on my neck and arms. Choosing a long-sleeved grey shirt and a beanie to help keep my hair down over my neck, along with color-correcting foundation spread generously over each bruise.

Deme is up and moving around. It has been ages since we woke up at the same time, and I sit on my bed to listen to her for a while; she turns on her music first, some pop song I can't make out. Dresser drawers open and close, she is picking out her outfit for today, she never wears the same outfit twice, and I haven't an inkling as to how she has the money for that. I, for sure, don't make that kind of money, and Dad spends most of his paycheck on beer.

I make breakfast and set the table while watching the news while I wait for Deme to come downstairs and join me. Everything is normal. Nothing interesting ever happens around here. The news anchor interviews a local baker, and they chat about a new bakery opening on Friday. I feel bad, most locally-owned businesses close after a year. Paradise is a tourist town; businesses depend on tourists to keep them in business. But winters are harsh here, and often, most of them close down before summer even starts. There are four other coffee shops in town other than the one I work at, ours is the only locally owned one, but most days, we barely make enough to cover labor costs.

"Anything interesting going on?" Deme asks, making her way into the kitchen.

"Nope, it's the same thing every day, Pinky." I laugh. Deme grabs a bagel from the counter.

"Are you feeling all right?" She asks, "I heard you tossing and turning all night."

"Yeah, I'm fine. I couldn't get comfortable." I tell her.

"So, it had nothing to do with Areon? Or Ty?" She raises an eyebrow.

"No, why would it?" I look back to breakfast and stir the eggs in front of me.

"Because you talk in your sleep." She tells me. I forgot I did that.

"No, I don't." I lie.

"Yes, you do. After Phoenix ran away, you talked in your sleep for months." She butters her bagel.

"I don't know what you're talking about."

"Fine," She drops the butter knife in the sink and turns to go out the door. "I'll see you at school then."

"Deme, wait, I—" I'm interrupted by a car honking.

"That should be Andrew. Like I said, I'll see you at school." Deme smirks and disappears in the hallway. I sigh in defeat and head out the door.

"Hey, Rose!" Gabby beams from the middle seat in Andrew's truck; this is new.

"Hey," I slide into the truck and put my bag under my seat. I close the door and stare out of the window; the truck doesn't move. "We'll be late again if you don't drive the truck, Andrew," I tell him.

"I want to make sure we're okay after I ditched you at the party the other night." He says and apologizes. He's sincere about it, but I'm not mad at him. Nothing about that night was his fault. He didn't even know what had happened, and as much as I want to be mad at him, I can't.

"I'm not mad at you if that's what you're asking," I say.

"Are you sure?" he asks, dragging this out more than he needs.

"I wasn't mad then, and I'm not mad now," I tell him.

"Good, I don't think I'd handle losing my best friend well." He smiles at me before putting the truck in drive and pulling out of my driveway.

I stare out the window, a group of kids is waiting by the mailbox to be picked up by the bus; one of them flips me off. Gabby and Andrew laugh about something, but I have no idea what they're talking about.

"Do you remember that, Rose? When you pushed that kid down the hill and didn't even get into trouble." She asks, I stared at her for a minute, trying to bring myself to remember but I can't. I look down at my hands, and Andrew clears his throat.

"She doesn't. I mean, it was so long ago I can't even believe I remember it." He says.

"What do you mean? It was only like six years ago." She asks. I look back at Andrew, waiting to hear what he'll tell her.

"Rose doesn't remember anything from when we were kids." He explains.

"Andrew," I warn.

"You really don't remember?" Gabby asks, looking at me. This is what I was trying to avoid. The pity. The look on her face says it all.

I slouch into the seat, "No, I don't."

"But her therapist said she would... one day," Andrew adds. I glare at him.

"You will?" A spark of hope shows on her face.

"No. The memories might come back one day, or they might not. Something needs to trigger the memory, and it'll come back. But that might never happen." I explain. I hate talking about it, and I'm surprised that Jessica never told her.

"What made you lose your memories in the first place?" She asks. Andrew's face goes blank. He wants to know if I'll tell her the same thing that I told him.

I told Andrew that I fell and hit my head. I blamed it on a concussion that I never got, but I could always tell that he didn't believe me. I wanted to tell Gabby the same thing, that it was a concussion that caused the memory loss, but it seems pointless. I'm lying about too many things now.

"I have Dissociative Amnesia," I start, "Some stressful experiences are so overwhelming and traumatic, the memories hide like a shadow in the brain. Sometimes, the memory returns within a few days or slowly, sometimes not at all. In my case, my memory returned slowly and then not at all. At first, my parents would show me pictures of myself and my classmates, drawings I had done, even home videos of me growing up. I remembered my name and who I was, and the things I had learned. I remembered everything I learned in school first and then re-learned the faces of my friends, but everything else was a blank. Memories are tricky to recover, and most doctors don't even recommend trying to get your memory back because there is the chance you could recover a false memory that will make you worse." The car is silent as I explain everything.

"Do you remember what the event was that caused it?" Gabby questions.

"Nope. The last thing I remember was being in the woods behind my house. Everything else is gone."

We get separated into groups in the first hour to work on a project on the Ancient Greeks. We have to come up with a board game based on Greek Mythology. Andrew, Areon, and I get partnered in the same group as each other, along with another girl named Breanne. Andrew and her start spit-balling ideas while Areon and I listen. After our conversation in the truck this morning, I feel better for telling the truth, but I could tell that Andrew is more than a little hurt I had lied to him for so long. I know I shouldn't have lied to him, but I don't know what happened in the forest; for all I know, I could've been hit on the head.

We settle on a game based around the board game "Monopoly," which we renamed to "Greekopoly," and everyone works on the layout for the entire game. Breanne is good at drawing, so she takes on drawing each of the cards. Areon still hasn't said anything to any of us, he listens to everything we say and nods, so we know he is listening. Halfway through the class, everyone in the room gets sidetracked from the assignment and starts talking about other things. Mr. Daniels doesn't seem to care that no one is working. He told us on the first day of the class that our grade was reflected by the work we did, and if we didn't want to work, then it wasn't his fault if we got the bad grade.

Our group is the only one still working on the assignment, but I can't focus. Everyone is talking about the party, and my ears can't help but listen in.

Everyone was talking about what they did during and after the party, but the group next to us is talking about something that happened today. It is hard to make out what they are saying because they are whispering to each other, but, from what I can hear, they are talking about Tyler. I hadn't seen him this morning, but apparently, he was beaten up. They didn't say what was wrong with him, but he at least had a black eye, and he wasn't telling anyone what had happened to him. Areon is watching me. I can't read his expression. I look down at my paper, pretend to work on it, and try to listen to more of the other groups, but no one is talking about the party anymore. Almost everyone has gone back to work besides Areon and me.

When the bell rings, everyone rushes to head out the door, but I stay behind to try to talk to Areon. I want to see if he's okay, or if for some reason, see if he is mad at me. I wait by the door for him, but he doesn't even look at me.

"Hey, Areon. Wait up." I hurry after him down the hall, and he slows down for me to catch up.

"You did a good job of covering up." He says.

"Yeah, but that's not what I wanted to talk to you about," I tell him.

"Yeah? Then, what's up?" he doesn't look at me; instead, he scans everyone around us. I'm still not sure if he can read minds.

"Are you okay?" I ask.

"I'm Fine."

"Okay...But you seem off today. Are you sure you're all right?" Areon stops walking abruptly, and I almost run into him, "Areon?" My eyes drift to what he is staring at. Tyler leans against his locker, talking to some of his friends. He is wearing a splint on his arm, and he has a black eye. "Areon. What happened?" I asked quietly. He grabs my arm and spins me to meet his face. It takes everything in me not to wince in pain as his fingers dig into one of my bruises.

"Look, me and you—" He gestures toward the both of us, "We aren't friends, and we can't be friends." His expression is hard as stone, he means it. I don't know how to respond, and I must look like a deer in the headlights.

"Hey, Rose!" I hear from behind me, but I still don't move. Deme inserts herself between Areon and me.

"Hey, Dem." I am still frozen in place; she has the worst timing.

"Hi, I'm Deme! Rose's sister; and you are?" She goes to shake hands with Areon.

"Areon," He says flatly.

"Oh!" Deme looks at me and smiles, then looks back at Areon, "She has told me so much about you already. It's nice to finally meet you." I could've hit her, but thankfully, I'm saved by the bell.

"Well, I guess I've got class; I'll see you guys later!" She winks at me and begins bouncing off in the opposite direction from us. Areon stares at me for a few seconds, I can tell he is searching for the right words to say, but I don't give him the chance to find them.

"Well, I'll see you around, I guess." I shrug and start walking away.

Gabby joins Andrew and me for lunch. They must've really hit it off at the party for them to be spending so much time together. I make a mental note to ask him about it later. I don't contribute to their conversation. I'm too lost in my own head, trying to figure out why Areon is treating me like this. One second, he cares about me, and the next, we can't even be friends? I can't remember a time I was so confused by someone.

"So, Rose, I was thinking." Gabby starts, leaning across the table to make eye contact with me. "How did you start remembering things after you lost your memory?" She asks.

"I mean, therapy, school, pictures, and home videos helped the most. So, I guess it was a visual thing?" I tell her.

"Okay, so pictures." She taps her fork to her mouth a few times, "Did you ever get those yearbooks from elementary school?"

"No, I don't think so." I didn't even know they made them.

"Well, I have all of them, you can borrow them if you want. Maybe they'll help you remember?" She smiles.

"Sure, it's worth a shot." I'm not sure if she is being nice for Andrew's sake or if it's just because she is a nice person. Either way, I appreciate the gesture.

"Okay, awesome, I'll drop them off at your house after school then!" she says excitedly.

"Actually, I have work after school. Do you think you could drop them off there?" I ask.

"Yeah! Common Grounds, right? I love the coffee there. And Jessica works tonight too, so I'll get to see you both!" Oh yeah, Jessica and Gabby are best friends.

"Yep, that's the place." I catch sight of Areon out of the corner of my eye. He is walking towards the tables that looked out over the courtyard, and part of me wants to invite him to sit with us but can't bring myself to do it. I don't want a repeat of the embarrassment I felt earlier.

I need a nap. I'm so exhausted by today that I'm basically dragging my bag along the ground as I make my way to Andrew's truck. I notice Areon walking towards me and quicken my pace. I go straight for the spare key that Andrew hides in the wheel-well only to find that it isn't there, and Areon is closing in on me.

"Hey," He says timidly. Okay, breathe, Rose. Breathe.

"Yeah?" I cross my arms and lean against the truck. I sound more annoyed than nervous, thankfully.

"I'm sorry about this morning," I don't believe him, "I shouldn't have said what I did, and I'm sorry." He apologizes.

"I don't believe you." I challenge.

"Why not?" he takes a step back.

"Why should I? Everything that comes out of your mouth contradicts something that you said before. Like that you care about me. If you really cared about me, then you wouldn't have said that we were not friends." I'm upset, and I couldn't help but let the words slip out of my mouth. It might be the truth, but it comes out a lot harsher than I mean it to.

"Rose, I mean it." He tries reaching out for my arm, but I pull away.

"Hey, Rosey!" Andrew beams as he walks up to the truck, "Oh, hey Areon." Areon nodded at him. "Are you ready to go, Rose?"

"Definitely." I glare at Areon and get into the passenger seat.

"See you, Areon." Andrew waves, getting into the car as Areon walks away.

"So, what happened back there?" Andrew asks as we drive towards my house. We haven't said a word to each other since we left the high school parking lot.

"Nothing, it doesn't matter," I tell him.

"If you insist." Andrew isn't the type to push, and he knows I'll tell him eventually.

"So, what's with you and Gabby? I'm assuming that went well?" I ask him, his cheeks redden.

"Yeah, it went amazing." He smiles from ear to ear as he tells me everything about the party: how she didn't care that his best friend is a girl, how they snuck away from everyone at the bonfire, and had their first kiss behind the barn. For some reason, I feel jealous.

"I have to admit, she's a lot nicer than I assumed she would be," I tell him.

"Yeah, I am sorry for ditching you, though." He says.

"Don't be," I say, even though I don't mean it.

"Well enough about what I did at the party, what did you do?" He asks. I can feel the heat leave my body. Could I tell him about Tyler, or about Areon? Or should I lie and tell him that I had a wonderful time? Silence fills the truck as I try to figure out what to tell him. Is telling him the truth worth it? "Did something bad happen?" He asks. In the side mirror, I look as white as a ghost.

"I don't really remember, honestly," I tell him as we pull into my driveway.

"Is it because of the memory thing, or did you black out from drinking?" I can't tell him the truth. He would tell someone, or worse, he would make *me* tell someone what happened.

"Maybe a little of both? I'll tell you when I remember." I joke, his mood lightens.

"Alright, well, this is your stop. Do you want me to take you to work? I could go for a coffee in a little bit." He asks.

"Yes, please, my legs are killing me. I don't think I could walk if I wanted to." I tell him.

I wake up from my nap feeling a million times better than I had this morning. I fix my hair and touch up the makeup on my bruises before putting my beanie back on to help keep them covered and head downstairs. My dad is at home. His truck is in the driveway, and while I'm fixing myself a sandwich, he comes inside and washes his grease-covered hands.

"How was your day today?" He asks, there is no hint of alcohol on his breath. Maybe he actually is going to keep his promise.

"It was alright, not over yet," I say between bites. I'm devouring this sandwich, and my stomach growls for more as I finish it.

"Actually, I was thinking." He pauses and looks at me funny, "Maybe you should quit that job over at the coffee place and focus on school right now."

"What? Why?" I protest.

"I've heard you moving around a lot in the middle of the night lately, and it doesn't seem like you've been getting a lot of sleep lately. I want to make sure that you're okay and that you're keeping up on your schoolwork." Is he trying to trick me? He seems sincere, but I've never seen heard him talk like this.

"What about money?"

"What about it? You're too young to worry about money." He tells me.

"Someone has to pay for Dem's expensive clothes, and make sure we have food on the table," I say and expect him to be angry, but he smiles instead of yelling.

"That's something for me to worry about, and I plan on being around for you girls from now on. I'm going to be sober, and I'm going to take care of you both." He is telling the truth. I'm not sure how I know this exactly, but he is sincere. I haven't heard him sound like this since mom died.

"Thank you." I don't know what happened to cause this change in him, but it feels like a weight has suddenly lifted off my shoulders. I squeeze his hand and realize that he is staring at my neck. I quickly turn and go to make another sandwich before he can ask me about the bruises. If he really is going to start acting like a good father, I don't want his first matter-of-business to be hunting down who beat his daughter up.

Work is slow. Mondays can be one of our busiest days because—well because it's Monday, but we've only had one customer since I got here. Andrew dropped me off, grabbed a coffee, and left almost two hours ago. I have also already restocked and cleaned everything in the entire store twice since I'd been here and am now making my third round to clean around the shop, so I look busy. I send Jess home and tell her I'll call if I need her to come back. She is more than happy not to work.

I try not to think about how much free time I'll have when I quit. It isn't like my grades are bad, but I am behind in a few classes because I didn't have enough time to do some of the essays I was assigned. I'm sure I would miss being here, though, as much as I hate the smell of coffee, I know that I will miss it when I don't get to be here all the time. Maybe I could ask for fewer shifts and work a few days of the week instead of every weekday.

I am in the middle of making a pros and cons list when the door chime goes off and in walks Areon.

"Are you stalking me?" I ask, leaning against the counter.

"Nope, I just really like the coffee here." He smiles.

"Long black?" I ask, he nods, and I go to make his drink.

"So, are you be able to talk?" he asks.

"We're talking now," I state

"That's not what I meant. Can you sit down and talk to me? I think I should explain a few things." He says.

"Areon, I am too exhausted to keep doing this back and forth thing with you. And before you apologize, maybe think about it for longer than five hours before trying to do so." I hand him his coffee, and he pays without saying another word.

Gabby comes in a few hours later. Her long, blonde hair is flowing behind her, and she is carrying five yearbooks and a few binders.

"Hey, girl!" She smiles, dropping the books onto the counter, "So this is everything that I have. The folders have a bunch of newspaper clippings in them that my parents saved, and I thought they might help, so I brought them too."

"Okay, thank you! I really appreciate it." I tell her, she must have great parents to keep all this stuff for her.

"Oh, it was no problem. Anything to help a friend." She smiles, "Plus, I'm really craving a vanilla frap." She laughs.

"Oh, of course. It's on the house," I tell her.

"No, that's okay. I'll pay." She pulls her wallet out from her back pocket, but I shake my head at her.

"Don't even try, I got you." I turn to start making her drink when I'm startled by a loud crash from across the room, I turn around and see a coffee cup in pieces on the ground. Coffee is spreading over the floor, and I quickly jump to grab some paper towels. I cover the coffee so it won't spread while the customer continues to apologize for dropping the cup. I leave the paper towels to soak up the coffee and tell them not to worry about it before going back to making Gabby's drink.

Gabby takes off after I give her the drink, and I go back to cleaning up the coffee spill. I realize too late that the coffee is so hot that I didn't feel the glass cutting my hands as I picked it up. I am covered in blood and coffee. Areon is the only one left in the lobby now. I know he is watching me though, so I try to hide my bloody hands from him and run to the back to wash up. Of course, the door chime goes off in the middle of me trying to stop the bleeding.

"I'll be with you in a minute!" I call out.

"Don't worry. It's me, Rose," Andrew announces, I sigh in relief. I quickly wrap up my hands and gather all the books and folders to give to Andrew to put in his truck when I realize that Andrew and Areon are having a full-on conversation. I guess there is a first for everything. I decide to leave them be and focus on closing.

Areon leaves the shop without me noticing, and Andrew helps me finish closing up the store.

"Thanks for coming tonight, I'd be screwed without you." I lock the front door.

"No prob. What did you do to your hands?" He asks.

"Some customer dropped his coffee mug, and it shattered," I explain as we get unto his truck.

"So, you weren't careful picking it up?"

"I mean, I was. I guess the coffee was just too hot for me to notice the glass cutting my hands." I tell him.

"Wait, what?" He asks, starting the vehicle.

"What do you mean, what?"

"You said the coffee was so hot that you didn't feel the glass cutting you. That doesn't make sense; weren't most of the orders to go? I thought you said earlier that no one else came in after Areon." I think it over for a minute. He's right. The coffee should've been lukewarm if not room temperature, and we keep the shop cool to try to keep people from loitering.

"The only way his coffee would've been hot enough was if he put it into the microwave or something, and I would've noticed." I pause, "I don't know, maybe I didn't notice. It's been a really long day, and I didn't get enough sleep last night."

"That's understandable," he says. We drive down the main highway, passing almost no one on the way to my house.

"So, what did you and Areon talk about?" I ask.

"Not a lot, I asked him if he ever went to the party. But he didn't really want to talk about it. He actually wanted to talk about you." He tells me.

"Oh, what did he want to know?" I ask.

"All your secrets." He laughs, "No, for real, though. Nothing really, I think he has a crush on you or something." My cheeks get warm, and I turn away from Andrew to hide my blushing. We talk about nothing the rest of the way home.

The house smells amazing. My nose leads me to the kitchen, where I find Dad and Deme laughing over the oven. Deme is stirring something in a pot while dad pours some kind of seasoning into it. Garlic smells flood my nose. Deme turns and finds me smiling at them.

"I thought I heard you come in." She smiles, "Take your shoes off and stay a while." I put my stuff down on the counter and clear off the table before taking a seat. I can't remember the last time I had dad cooking; he was always better at it than mom, but I would never tell her that. I feel my heart sink. I can't even remember the last time we ate a meal as a family. All of us, mom and Phoenix included. I hope this won't be the last time we all eat together, but I try not to let my poor faith ruin the moment. My stomach growls. I've eaten more than my fair share of food today, but nothing has been able to satisfy my hunger.

"So, how was work?" My dad asks, he hands Deme some bowls to set out on the table.

"Slow, I cut my hands pretty badly," I tell him.

"How'd you do that?" He asks.

"Someone dropped a glass, and I didn't notice the glass pieces cut me when I picked them up," I explain.

"So, that's why you have bandages on your hands." He says, although I don't know how he noticed, he hasn't looked at me since I walked in the kitchen. Mom used to say they had eyes on the back of their heads. I laugh at the memory.

"Yeah," I tell him.

"Why don't you go take them off and let the cuts breathe a little bit and wash up for dinner."

"Yeah, Rose. And take a shower, you smell of something, and it ain't roses." Deme winks at me, "Dinner should be ready soon." She adds and stirs to the pot again, "We're making mom's chili recipe, she always said that the longer it cooks, the better it tastes. So, take your time if you need it."

I get out of the shower and wrap a towel around myself before stepping out into the freezing air; Deme must've turned the AC on. I'll have to reapply the makeup to my bruises before I head back downstairs, but I don't mind. At this point, I'm used to having to spend extra time getting ready. I comb through my hair with my fingers before realizing that my hair could get caught in the cuts. I look down at them, and I can't believe my eyes. I turn my hands over, and all the cuts are gone, not even a trace of them left behind. Shocked, I pull my hair up into a ponytail and check the bruises, they're gone too. The ones on my arms and legs have disappeared as well. In fact, every bruise or scar that I have ever gotten has vanished from my skin. They were there this morning. It isn't possible that they would just be gone over a few hours, so what happened?

"Rose!" Deme shouts from downstairs, "Hurry up, we're starving down here!"

"I'll be down in a minute!" I yell back.

Okay, breathe. Just breathe. I need to hold it together during dinner, no need to ruin this night. I change into pajamas quickly and braid my hair before heading downstairs. Hopefully, this is a good thing. Deme won't have a reason to freak out if I don't have the bruises anymore.

Eating dinner and hanging out with them makes me nostalgic for the old times. But I still can't help but feel like Dad is going to turn back into the alcoholic that we'd grown used to. I can't tell if Deme feels the same way that I do, but if she does, she's hiding it well. Dad, on the other hand, is showing no signs that he has been drinking at all. I can't even smell it on him like I used to be able to. It feels like we are a family again. Smiling and laughing. Dad's making fun of us like he used to. For the first time in forever, we are actually enjoying each other's company.

"Hey Rose, did you happen to see what happened to Ty at the party the other night?" Deme asks, my heart sinks. She had to catch me off guard, didn't she? I immediately feel my father's eyes on me. Deme is acting like it was nothing. I feel like I am about to get into trouble, like I'm still a kid and might get spanked for doing something wrong, but I'm not a kid anymore, and I somehow know that Dad wouldn't say anything about it.

"Nope," I'm not lying, "I have no idea what happened. Why?"

"Oh, he said the last thing that he remembers was hanging out with you, but he was probably too drunk to even remember correctly." She says nonchalantly.

"Yeah, maybe." My eyes divert to the pile of yearbooks I put on the counter, "I think I'm going to go upstairs and go through those books until I'm tired. Gabby gave them to me so I could see if they triggered any memories. Maybe it'll work." I can tell that my dad and Deme aren't done hearing about the party, but they don't say anything until I grab the books and head for the door.

"Can I come look through them with you? I love going through old yearbooks." Deme asks.

"Yeah, of course." I motion for her to follow.

My eyes start to drift closed; going through yearbooks from elementary school isn't the most exciting activity. I haven't remembered anything so far, and Deme isn't helping any. She barely flipped through the first yearbook before she started scrolling through her phone.

"What do you think happened to Ty?" Deme asks, my eyes snap open.

"I'm not sure, maybe he fell or got into a fight, maybe both? I don't know." I tell her.

"Are you sure you don't know?" I wish she would drop this.

"Yes, I'm sure, Deme, I honestly have no idea." I sigh.

"Well, I mean. With your bruises and his broken arm, maybe something happened that you don't want to remember? Maybe something bad, that caused you to lose your memory again?" I stare at her. Why would she think that I lost my memory again? I'm not acting the way I had when I lost it the first time, and I clearly remembered everything that happened that night before I blacked out. It's just the Tyler part that I don't remember.

"No, Deme, I didn't lose my memory. And look—" I pull the braid away from my neck, "—No bruises. I'm fine." I tell her.

"Okay, okay, I believe you." She looks back down at the yearbook and flips through a few more pages.

After going through two more yearbooks, I am ready to call it quits. I turn my phone on to check for any new messages, but there aren't any. I'm ready for bed when Deme looks up at me.

"Rose? What's Areon's last name?" She asks.

"I can't remember, I think it starts with an 'L' maybe?" I tell her.

"And he moved here this year? He's never lived here before?" She asks.

"I'm sure someone would've remembered him. Why?" I ask, she's beating around the bush, and I'm too tired to entertain her questions any longer.

"You should look at this." Deme hands me the yearbook in her hands and points to a picture. I would've dropped the book if it wasn't resting in my lap already. There, in black and white, is a picture of Areon as a child.

The picture is haunting to look at. There is no expression on his face. No smile or certain look in his eyes. He looks dead inside. I suddenly feel sick to my stomach.

"Rose? Are you okay?" Deme asks.

I nod, "Yeah, I'm just really confused. Are there any other pictures of him in here?"

"Not that I noticed. Check the index." She tells me. I flip to the back of the book and find the last name 'Lux' in the long list. There are only two pages that he is on, one of which is the portrait that we have already seen, so I flip through the pages until I get to the other one. I gasp.

No way.

There is absolutely no way.

Deme scoots closer, trying to find what shocked me.

"What the hell?" She says, "That's you and Andrew! Is that other kid Areon?" I nod slowly; I can't believe my eyes. It's a picture of us as children, standing on the playground. The picture is right in front of me, and I can't believe it. Andrew doesn't remember

Areon, and he doesn't even like Areon now. How could we have been friends with him and not remember? I have a good excuse, but Andrew would have to have a really good one not to remember this.

"You should definitely ask them both about this tomorrow. Why would someone move back and pretend like they didn't know anyone? This doesn't make sense." Deme is excited, her voice full of energy. I feel weak. Every ounce of energy drained from my system the second I saw this picture. I know that my brain is trying to remember Areon. I felt this drained all the time when I first lost my memory. But, almost immediately, I would remember and would be fine again. This feels different like something isn't allowing me to remember.

I sneak out of the house after Deme falls asleep. I called Andrew and told him to come to pick me up down the road from my house. I'm not sure if Andrew will believe me or not, but I need to tell him. He was there with us in the picture, and he never lost his memory, so he should be able to remember Areon, let alone us taking a picture with him when we were kids.
I walk in the dark for what feels like forever. It feels like one of those dreams where you can't reach the end of the hallway, no matter how fast you run toward it. When I finally reach the mailbox at the end of my street, everything in me says to turn back.

Something is coming, or about to happen; I'm not sure what, but I can feel it in my bones. Andrew is taking his sweet time, so I sit under a tree by the stop sign and wait. The night is silent, no dogs bark in the distance, no wind flows through the trees. Leaves rustle on the ground behind me, and I turn to look, but there's nothing but darkness. I look up at the sky, the moon hides behind the clouds making it even darker out. I can't see anything. The leaves rustle again, but still, I can't see anything. I feel even worse than I did before; like something or someone is watching me.

Then I hear it.

A loud growl from behind me makes me freeze in place. Slowly, I turn my head and find myself face-to-face with a coyote. My heart pounds. It is so close that I could pet it, but I don't move or break eye contact. We stare at each other, neither of us breaking eye contact, I am too afraid to. This is how dogs show dominance; if I look away, it is sure to attack me.

"It's okay, pup. I'm not going to hurt you," I whisper, it backs up a step and growls again before yipping. I slowly lift myself onto my feet. Being sure to keep my shoulders square with his and maintaining eye contact. The coyote lunges forward at me, and I fall back. It stands on my chest while it smells me. I am shaking and can hear my heartbeat.

The coyote steps away from me, lowering its head as it moves away. It looks like its bowing. I lift myself back up. The coyote is at least ten feet away from me now. I don't understand why it is backing off me, but I'm thankful. Without warning, it takes off, running into the darkness and out of sight. I stand up and brush myself off. That is the most bizarre thing that has happened to me. I can't wrap my head around it. I don't think I can handle being out here another minute; hopefully, Andrew will be here soon. I start pacing to try to work the adrenaline out of my system. That's when I hear a deeper growl.

I get hit by something hard. I feel it in my back first, like something has stabbed straight through the lower part of my spine and popped it out of place. It's enough to drop me to the ground and knock the wind out of me. I try to stand up, but my body feels like it has been set on fire. I am itchy everywhere. It starts on my arms and spreads like wildfire. Then I realize that I am growing hair all over. Thick patches spread over my arms and up onto my hands, then down my back and onto my legs. What is happening? I can't wrap my head around it, and the stabbing in my back progressively gets worse until it feels like I am paralyzed. My ribs pop in and out of place, and that's when I can't stand the pain anymore. I scream louder than I ever have. I didn't even know I could make that sound. My ribs continue to shift, then my joints, every bone in my body feels like it is breaking. It's like my body has become one giant charley-horse. I lay on the ground, screaming in pain, hoping that someone will come find me and help me. I start to black out. My body is undoubtedly unable to process the amount of pain coursing through it. Certain that whatever is happening is going to kill me, I close my eyes, embrace the pain, and try relaxing on the ground.

As instantly as it had started, everything stops. The world is silent. My skin and bones aren't on fire anymore, but I feel different. I feel smaller and more agile. My senses are heightened too. A fire burns in the distance. Something has died here recently. It's like my sense of smell is eight-hundred times stronger than before. I hear a car approaching and look around, it has to be Andrew. Sure enough, his truck pulls around the corner and parks on the side of the road, the light of his phone reflects on his face. I look but have no idea where my phone is.

"Rose?" He whispers, getting out of his truck. I want to respond and tell him that I am right here, but I can't speak. Almost like I don't know how to anymore. Every time I try, I make a whimpering sound instead. Andrew walks towards where I am but stops a few feet away from me. He looks like he is paralyzed in fear. I don't understand. He is looking right at me but isn't saying anything or moving a muscle. I look behind me to see what he is looking at, but there's nothing there. I turn back around, as Andrew starts to back up towards his truck.

"Easy, pup, I'm not going to hurt you." He says. Is he talking to me? Why did he call me a pup? Is the coyote still around? I inch forward towards him, a little way out of the shadows. "It's okay, I'm going to get into my truck and drive away. I promise I won't hurt you." He says. What the hell? I'm not going to hurt him, and why would he even think that I would? I step out of the shadows and into the moonlight, that's when I see my shadow.

I'm a wolf. My shadow is unmistakable. I am a wolf with four legs and a tail, and I'm giant. I turn around as Andrew gets into the truck, I take a step back. He is afraid of me. I mean, he doesn't know it is me, but still, he is afraid. I feel like a monster as I skulk back into the shadows. As he drives off, I lay under the tree I first sat under, watching his taillights disappear down the road.

4

The Woods

I'm running. Faster and faster.

With every step, I'm gliding over the earth like I'm flying. The trees and bushes blur past me. I feel wild and more alive than I ever have before. I make my way through the woods like I had every day before this. Every inch of the forest is etched in my brain, like a map that only I can see. I turn sharply, heading towards the middle of the forest. He will be waiting there for me, in the same spot that we meet every day to play with each other.

I slow my pace down as I get closer. Something is wrong. I smell something that I have never smelled in my life. It smells like rotten meat with a mix of cheap perfume. It is horrid. As I near the source of the smell, I can't help but bury my nose in the dirt, it makes me want to vomit. The dirt helps mask the scent, but it is still overwhelming. I close in, the scent comes from the fort we'd made, and I feel a knot in my stomach. Is he okay? There are crows everywhere. As I inch closer to the fort, they don't even scatter away from me. Something is dead in here, and they want it. I see him. His body is still, and I can't hear him breathing. I run to him, but there is no use, I can tell by the smell of his body that he is dead. He has no wounds. The only thing out of order on him is that his mouth is open, and on his tongue rests a peculiar silver coin. Areon is dead.

I turn and run for home; my heart beats a million beats per minute. He is dead, and he is never going to come back. What had happened to him, though? Was it my fault? I should've been there with him; I am the protector, after all. I am supposed to keep him safe, and I failed. My mind races, and, all at once, I lose my way. The forest becomes unfamiliar and terrifying. I trip over the roots of a tree and land on my side. I feel a slight pain in my side and realize that I have turned back into a human. I lay my head on the ground and start crying.

I wake up gasping for air, tears roll down my cheeks. I look around, lost. I'm home in bed. Had I been dreaming about everything? No, that was too real to be a dream. But if it wasn't a dream, then how did I get back home? I stand up, but something stops me in my tracks.

I remember.

I remember everything that has ever happened to me. I remember my classmates from school that don't even live here anymore. I remember the family vacations in Mexico that we used to go on. And I remember the fort in the forest that Andrew, Areon, and I had built as children. I remember Areon. I sit back down, dizzy, and nauseous.

I was a wolf, and Areon was dead.

I saw him with my own two eyes. I remember it like yesterday. I can see it so clearly in my head that it doesn't make any sense. Why had I suddenly remembered everything? Am I going to lose them again? Will anyone believe me?

The doorbell rings, I look at my phone on the bedside table. I am late. Andrew probably got sick of waiting for me and came to the door. I start making my way downstairs when I hear the door open.

"Good morning, Mr. Knight. Is Rose ready to go?" Andrew's voice is shaky. He is terrified of my dad, hence calling him mister.

"No, she won't be going today. She isn't feeling well." My dad says sternly as I walk slowly down the staircase. When I get to the bottom of the stairs and turn the corner, I can tell how uneasy Andrew feels by looking at him. He relaxes when he sees me.

"Oh yeah, you don't look so good. Alright, then, I guess I'll see you later." He turns and heads to his truck, I don't get to see him make it there though because my dad shuts the door and turns to face me.

"Dad, I—" I start. He shakes his head; he doesn't want to hear it.

"I have to call your school, and then we'll talk." He says, heading towards the kitchen, "And you're quitting your job today. Now, go upstairs and shower, you smell like a wet dog."

For the first time in a long time, I am terrified of my father. I have grown up and gotten used to him being drunk all the time, which made him a jerk, but I never thought he was terrifying before. Sure, he'd go on rampages and destroy plates or other things in the house, but he never took out his anger on us. I don't think he's yelled at either Deme or me since Phoenix had run away; this feels different. He is so calm that it scares me. I don't know what he is doing or why he called me out of school. Did he know that I snuck out? Did I do something that I couldn't remember that upset him? I have no idea.

We sit at the kitchen table in silence, and I can tell he is searching for the words to say to me. My skin crawls with anticipation. I'm expecting him to yell, to scream maybe. If he really knew that I snuck out, he'd be livid.

"Dad—" I start, but he shushes me. I can't sit in silence anymore, though; this feels like torture. I scratch at my skin and look down at my arms. There is no trace of the fur that once covered my body. Maybe it was just a dream. One second, I was me, and then next, I was an animal. That isn't possible. It felt so real, though. So, would that make me a werewolf? There are so many things running through my head that I almost don't hear when my dad finally speaks.

"Rose, I know what happened last night." He says, and I slouch down into my chair, he knows that I snuck out. This is it; I am going to be in trouble. I don't understand why he's going to punish me, though. How could he expect me to go back to normal after years of taking care of myself? I was a good kid who got good grades, and I basically raised Deme, so why would he think that, after a few days, he could go back to being a good father?

"Dad, I'm sorry I snuck out, but—" I start to say, but he quiets me again.

"I don't care about that, Rose." He says. I don't understand.

"Rose, last night, you turned into a wolf. There's no easy way to say it, so I have to be blunt." He takes a deep breath, "You are part wolf. Which would technically mean you are a werewolf. I noticed yesterday that your bruises had disappeared and assumed the cuts on your hands would as well because you were going to turn." He waits for a response from me, but I stay quiet. "I know you must have some questions, and there might be a few that I can't answer, but I will try the best I can to answer all of them."

"How?" I ask, almost immediately, "How is that possible?"

"It runs in your blood; you and Phoenix inherited the gene from me. You have had it your whole life; Only when you lost your memory, you lost the ability to transform."

"And now that I have my memory back, I can turn," I whisper; his eyes widen.

"You got your memories back? When?" he asks.

"Last night. After I turned, I guess." I tell him.

"The trauma of the turn must've made you remember. Do you remember when you lost your memory?" He asks. Areon's lifeless body flashes in my memory. I nod.

"I saw a dead body in the forest. I was running home to come tell you and mom, but I didn't make it." We sit in silence for a few moments. Dad doesn't look at me, but I stare at him, waiting for him to tell me more. When he doesn't say anything, I finally ask the question that has been on my mind, "Did mom know?"

"Did mom know what?" He shifts in his seat uncomfortably and glances at the fridge.

"That you're a wolf," I say.

"Yes, she knew that I was a wolf. But I can't turn anymore." He tells me, turning his attention back to me.

"You can't?" I ask.

"No. When your brother was born, I went through a trial. Male wolves are different, we can't control ourselves like the females can. Women can turn completely; men have to learn control before we can completely transform. We are stuck between man and beast. This trial allowed me to give up the wolf form permanently, it was too dangerous for me to be around a newborn baby. Although, I did get to keep some perks, I still have stronger senses than a human normally would. The alcohol numbs them a bit." He tries to smile, but the pain in his eyes clouds it. "Rose, I'm sorry," his voice begins to shake, "There are going to be some things that you will have to get used to. Smells you wont be able to un-smell, whispered words that you wont be able to un-hear." Tears swell in his eyes and I have to fight back my own.

"When your mother got sick, I could... I could sense when she was getting worse and I couldn't take it. I'm sorry, I should've been there for you." My heart is racing, but I remain still. As if any movement will prevent my father from speaking. "Even through the alcohol, I knew there was a change coming. Knowing you would transform again, knowing you would need me again, is the reason I stopped drinking. I won't leave you again, I promise I will be here for the two of you from now on." I reach for my fathers hand across the table as silent tears stream down my face. He squeezes my hand gently as he fights back tears of his own. "Is there anything else you wanna ask me?" He asks quietly.

"Will turning always be that painful?" I ask. He laughs at me.

"Until you get used to it, it will be that painful for a while. The last time you changed was when you were still a child. You've gone longer than most without turning, and it will take a toll on you. Which is how I found you and why I called you out of school." He explains.

"You heard me screaming, didn't you?" I ask.

"Yeah, any wolf in a fifty-mile radius would've heard you." He says.

"How come no one else did, though? There were houses with lights on and—" I cut myself off, not wanting to bring up Andrew.

"Because you weren't really screaming, you were howling. No one would have been brave enough to find out why you were howling." He tells me.

"What!?" There was no way I was howling. I heard myself scream.

"Calm down, I know what you're thinking. The voice is one of the first things that go during the transformation." He says.

"That doesn't make any sense, though, I heard myself screaming," I tell him.

"It's more like thinking; only you can hear your thoughts, but you still sound like yourself." He says.

"I don't get it." I rest my head in my hands. I have a headache.

"When you're a wolf, you don't have the ability to speak, so your thoughts take over, and only you can understand what you're trying to say. But, to anyone else, you'll sound like an animal." Dad explains.

"I guess that makes sense, but why, how are we wolves? That doesn't make sense to me. Werewolves are in old stories and movies; they aren't supposed to be real." I explained.

"Well, we are the descendants of the very first wolves." He clears his throat, "Long ago, there was a king, and he was an awful, horrid man. One day, a traveler in rags came to him and asked for hospitality from the king, but this was no ordinary traveler. He was the Greek God known as Zeus. The King recognized the God and decided to trick him. He killed his son and offered the meat from his bones to the God as a meal. However, Zeus caught on to his deception and turned the king and his other son into wolves and placed a type of curse on the people of the village."

"Wait, so you're telling me that, not only are we descendants of a king who was turned into a wolf but also that the Greek Gods really existed?" I interrupt him.

"Yes, the Gods exist. Every one of them." He tells me.

"So why are we being punished then? After all this time, couldn't he have lifted the curse and made us normal again?" I ask.

"Yes, but that's not how it works. Zeus required that each year, when people of the village became of age, they would undergo the Trial of the wolf. If they spent sixty days as a wolf and did not feed on human flesh, they would return to normal and go home, start a family, live a normal life until death. But if they fed on the flesh of man, they would spend the rest of their lives as a wolf." He explains to me.

"So that's what you did? The Trial of the Wolf?" I questioned.

"Yes and no. Things are a little different nowadays. All the descendants are free to transform whenever they please, so I guess you could say that we evolved as a species. But if one doesn't want to turn, then they must first make a sacrifice to Zeus, which is a chore to complete. If he accepts, then your trials begin on the night of the wolf moon." He tells me.

"So, Phoenix and I are wolves. What about Deme?" I ask.

"She did not inherit the wolf gene. She doesn't even know about it." He says.

"Why not?"

"Because we didn't know if you would ever be able to turn again, and your brother swore not to tell her. We thought it would be easier for you not to remember. I'm sorry we kept this from you."

"Are we going to tell her now?" I ask.

"It is up to you." He tells me.

I lie in bed for hours going over the conversation I had with my dad. Werewolf. Is that really what I am? A mythical creature? No, that sounds too narcissistic; I am a monster. I am glad I wasn't at school today; my body is sore. Dad said it would go away after the first few times of turning, but this felt worse than anything I'd felt after the party. I sit up, realizing that I never told Andrew what happened; and what about Areon? Does he know what I am? Speaking of, how is he even alive? A symptom of dissociative amnesia is false memories, is this one of them?

I grab my phone off the table—one missed call from Andrew, but he didn't leave me a voicemail. I text him quickly, saying sorry for this morning and that I need to talk to him later when he has a chance. He should be getting out of school soon. I get out of bed and grab some clothes from my dresser. I get dressed and go to head downstairs when my phone starts ringing.

"Hello?" I answer.

"Rose, what the hell happened at Craig's party?" Deme is yelling.

"I told you I don't know; why?" I ask.

"Because Tyler and Areon literally got into a fight over you." She tells me.

"What! Why?" I gasp.

"I don't know, they were in the parking lot leaving when Tyler went up to Areon and said something. I only caught the end of it when Areon hit Ty and said that if he ever said anything about you again, he'd kill him." She explains.

"Holy shit." I can't believe it, Areon had to have done something to him at the party, and Tyler remembered it even though he said he didn't.

"Are you sure you don't remember a thing?" Deme asks again.

"I mean, I might've gotten my memory back, but you can't remember what you didn't see." Silence. I check my phone to see if the call got disconnected when Deme finally responds.

"Wait, you got your memory back?" She asks quietly. I didn't tell her first; it probably hurt her feelings.

"Yeah, this morning. That picture triggered it, and everything came back. Dad is the only other person who knows. I'm sorry I didn't tell you first." I say.

"Wow, okay." She sighs, "It's okay, I believe you. But like, did you hear anything? Something that might have caused them to fight in the middle of the parking lot?" She asks.

I take a deep breath. "Tyler was messing with me and wouldn't leave me alone, Areon must've called him out on it or something. I don't know."

"Messing with you." She repeats, "Alright, I guess I'll talk to you later. Call your lover-boy and get all of this sorted." She tells me.

I blush, and I'm glad she can't see me, "Okay, I will. Love you, later."

"Love ya!" she shouts, and the line goes dead. Not even a minute later, my phone buzzes again, Andrew is on his way over to pick me up for work. Work. I'd completely forgotten. I look around my room for all of my aprons and gather them into a bag. Today is going to be my last day working at the coffee shop. I can't wait for today to be over.

Dad is hesitant to let me leave, but knowing he's forcing me to quit my job and skip school made him okay with letting me out. However, he fought me about who's going to drive me there. Andrew doesn't even come to the door, which I am okay with. I didn't want Dad to scare Andrew away. He doesn't relax until he pulls up to the stop sign at the end of the street.

"Where were you last night?" He asks me, turning the corner.

"Something happened to me that's going to be hard to believe, but I have to start from the beginning, okay?" I start. How in the world am I going to summarize what happened?

"Alright." He shoots me a look of confusion.

"You've never met Areon before, right?" I ask. I should start at the beginning.

"No, he moved here. How would I have met him before?" He says.

"Because he didn't just move here. Well, he did, but we were friends with him when we were children." I say.

"What? No, Rose, I've never met the guy in my life. I would've remembered him." He argues.

"I have a picture to prove it, Andrew," I tell him.

"How?"

"Those yearbooks, that Gabby gave me, there was a picture of the three of us together as children. That picture triggered my memory, and I remember everything like it was yesterday."

"Wait, you got your memory back? That's great!" Andrew yells.

"Yeah, but you're missing the point. We were friends with Areon as children, and now he's back." I say.

"Then, why don't I remember him? It's not like I lost my memory. I remember everything from my childhood. Why would I have forgotten him?" He has a point, why wouldn't he remember Areon? If we really were all best friends, he would have. Maybe he did something to make us lose our memory of him, it wouldn't be the strangest thing that I found out this week.

"Andrew, there's one more thing," I tell him.

"What's that?" he asks.

"The reason why you didn't see me last night," I take a deep breath, preparing myself for his disbelief, "The wolf you saw, that was me. I'm part wolf." Andrew slams on the breaks, and I have to grab on to the dashboard to avoid going through the windshield.

"What!?" He yells, a car behind us honks their horn before passing us and flipping us off. "Now, you're messing with me, you're lying. You're trying to freak me out. There's no way." He denies, trying to convince himself otherwise. He repeats himself more than once that I'm lying. I could try to convince him, but I know that, right now, he won't listen.

We don't say anything else as we pull into the Common Grounds parking lot. Andrew pulls into a spot and throws the truck into park. He is shaking. I want to convince him that what he saw was me, but how else would I have known about the wolf?

"Where's the picture?" He questions, catching me off guard.

"What?" I ask.

"You said that you have proof; I want to see the picture." He says, and I pull my phone out. I'd taken a picture of the page on my phone, but I wish I would've brought the yearbooks with me. "No way," he zooms in on the picture, "How do I not remember this, I don't even remember this picture being taken."

"Honestly, every memory I have that involves Areon is a little fuzzy to me too, almost like I was dreaming it. There's only one that I remember clearly, and it's from the day that I lost my memory in the first place." I tell him.

"What happened?" Andrew asks.

"Long story short, I was running through the forest to a fort that we built together, and when I got there, it smelled like death. Areon was dead inside." I explain Andrew all, but he loses it.

"Wait, he was dead? Maybe it's not Areon. People can't come back from the dead, Rose. That isn't possible. You're pranking me, aren't you?" he says.

"People aren't supposed to turn into wolves either, but I did last night," I tell him.

We head inside and sit at one of the booths, Jess is working already, but she doesn't seem incredibly happy about it, she seems more stressed than she usually does. I walk up to the counter, where she restocks the caramel and vanilla.

"Hey, Jess, you okay?" I asked.

"I'm great!" She fakes a smile, and I know that something is up. Her eyes dart to the office which could only mean one thing; the owner is here. John only comes in once every couple of weeks to put orders in and check through all the inventory. He hates being here as much as the rest of us do. I won't have a better time to quit. I head to the door, and before I can even knock, I hear his voice.

"Come in." John's voice calls from the other side of the door. I open it to find him with his face buried in a box of receipts, "What's up, Rose?"

"Hey, sorry to bother you, and I'm also really sorry about the short notice, but today's going to have to be my last day," I tell him.

"Excuse me?" he looks up, his brown eyes are filled with annoyance.

"I'm sorry, it's... I've fallen behind in my schoolwork, and my dad is upset about it. So, he's making me quit." I stutter.

"Fine, bring your keys in tomorrow." He says annoyed and turns back to his box of receipts.

"Oh, and Rose, put the help wanted sign out and close the door behind you. Thanks." I leave his office and shut the door behind me.

After putting the help wanted sign in the window, I sit down next to Andrew in a booth, Jessica follows behind me.

"You quit?" She asks.

"Yeah, I had to,"

"Oh, well, when is your last day then?" she asks.

"It's today," I tell her.

"Really, dang. Well, I'd say I would miss you, but I don't think I'll get rid of you this easy." Jessica sneers and turns on her heels to walk away from us.

"She is a horrible human being," I whisper to Andrew behind my hand.

"Yeah, but she's Gabby's best friend, so she has to have some good qualities." He shrugs.

"I guess so." I sip at my coffee. This is the first moment I feel like my life isn't a movie. Everything feels normal, just Andrew and I hanging out like we did before I found out I was a wolf, and that Gods existed and that Areon was dead. I close my eyes and take a deep breath; a week ago, it just smelled like coffee beans in here. Now, I could tell you every individual smell in the air. Cocoa, vanilla, cinnamon.

"Rose? You alright?" Andrew asks, I smile at him and nod.

"Yeah, I'm okay. I just have this feeling that everything is going to change. That when I walk out of this building, everything is going to be different from now on." I say.

"I mean, it already is." He's right. Before last night, I had no idea that I could turn into a wolf, and my dad was sure that my ability to was lost forever. If I never found that picture, I never would've remembered. "But you'll always have me. we'll be friends forever." Andrew adds.

"Don't be such a sap," I laugh and punch him in the shoulder playfully, "But, yeah. No matter what, we'll always have each other."

Andrew pulls me into him, his familiar warmth cocoons me. I feel safe.

Areon walks into the coffee shop halfway through my shift, almost right after Andrew left. I send Jessica out to take his order; she's more than happy to.

"You still going to come in here when Rose doesn't work here anymore?" Jess asks. I'm hiding around the corner, listening in.

"What are you talking about?" Areon questions, he sounds annoyed. Probably because she mentioned me and the last time we talked, I wasn't exactly nice to him.

"It's her last day today. I was trying to make a joke," Jessica says flatly. She started ringing him up on the register, the buttons beep in succession. "Same as usual?" She asks, but there's no response, I assume he nodded because, seconds later, I hear coffee pouring. I'm too nervous to talk to him. Instead, I stay hidden in my corner, taking deep breaths until John comes out to yell at me.

"I get that it's your last day and you don't care, but I do. If you want a good recommendation when you leave, then I would get back to work if I were you." He goes back to the office. I swallow my anxiety and walk to the front of the house. Areon sits where he usually does, his face buried in his laptop. I grab a bottle of 409 and spray down the counter, keeping my back to him. Jess pretends to be busy counting cups and moving things around.

Avoiding Areon is easy for the first few hours; a decent number of customers are coming in. It isn't until closing time, and people started trickling out the door that I have a harder time avoiding Areon's gaze. I sent Jess home almost right after John walked out for the week. He didn't even say anything nice to me before leaving, which is a little upsetting since I have worked here every weekday for the last year and a half, with only one raise barely a promotion. John was never really the type to say anything nice, though. It's a wonder that he is even married and with kids.

I finish counting inventory, restocking the shelves, and am waiting for the last five customers to leave when Areon locks eyes with me. He smiles and waves before going back to his laptop. Thirty more minutes before I can kick everyone out.

Finally, its closing time. I called for last drinks ten minutes ago, and everyone is already cleared out except for Areon. I start flipping the chairs onto the tables to prepare for mopping. As I do, Areon packs up his things into a black backpack.

"Hey, did you need a ride?" He asks. I need to talk to him, anyway, now is as good as never.

"Yeah, that would be great. Let me mop, lock up, and I'll be right out." I smile awkwardly as I flip a chair over. He walks out the front door silently, and I finish closing up after texting Andrew that I'll meet up with him later.

Areon waits for me at his jeep, holding the door for me as usual. He helps me in before climbing into his own seat and starting the car. I'm so nervous I visibly shake. I'm not sure I can hold back from saying anything to him any longer.

"Areon, I remember you," I say, catching him off guard. He almost runs a stoplight.

"Well, good. I mean, it would be pretty weird if you didn't." He chuckles. Of course he is going to play dumb. Why wouldn't he?

"No, I remember you from when we were children," I tell him.

"That is impossible, Rose. I just moved here." He says.

"Then, why are you so protective over me? And why did you get into a fight with Tyler over me today? And why do you show up everywhere that I am? And why did you go to the party in the first place?" I have word vomit. I can't stop asking questions, "And what did you do to Tyler on the night of the party? And why do I remember clearly finding your dead body in the middle of the woods behind my house when we were kids?"

"Woah-woah-woah, take it easy, girl." He says.

"You need to tell me the truth, Areon, the whole truth. I need to know." I tell him.

"Okay, fine. Not here. Let's go somewhere else." He says, turning down a side road.

We drive for a while, and I don't know what to talk about other than what he is waiting to tell me; it makes the drive agonizing. We drive past my house and further down the road. It's not until we hit a dirt road that I know where we are going.

"Why are we here?" I ask.

"Because we are going back where it all started." He tells me.

"Where what all started?" I ask.

"I'll tell you when we get there, okay?" He says.

"Okay, I guess." I hate this, and I feel uneasy, which is strange. This is the first time that I've felt unsafe with Areon.

"Why did you get into a fight with Tyler?" I ask, changing the subject.

"Because he said some things that weren't true about you." He explains.

"Like what?" I ask. I can't imagine it was anything good since it resulted in a fight.

"It really doesn't matter." He says.

"Just tell me, Areon." I sigh, I'm sick of this back and forth.

"He called you an unsavory name and said you slept together the night of the party. Which obviously wasn't true, and I couldn't stand to hear him tell lies anymore." He clenches his fists around the steering wheel, his knuckles turn white.

"Oh, well, thank you," I say.

"No problem," He says, loosening his grip on the steering wheel, "I didn't hurt him, by the way."

"What?" I ask.

"The night of the party, I know my strength, I never broke his arm." He explains.

"Then how do you suppose he broke it?" I ask, surprised that he's actually talking to me about Tyler.

"I don't know, all I know was that he tried to hurt you and I pulled him off and pushed him away. Unless he fell or got into another fight after that, then I'm not sure how he did." He tells me.

"Do you think he's faking it?" I ask.

"I don't know." He shrugs. "We never talked about what happened after, are you okay? How are the bruises feeling?"

"It honestly feels like the party was years ago, I'm fine. I don't even have the bruises anymore." Areon takes his eyes off the road and scans my neck, and then my arms. "Areon, please watch the road. I'm fine."

The headlights rest on a small building in the middle of a field. It's an old cottage that hasn't been lived in for at least thirty years. Kids we went to school with used to tell old ghost stories about it when we were younger. So, it's still here, after all. I get out of the jeep, not waiting for Areon, and walk up to the small building we used to play in when we were children. Only someone has been rebuilding it.

"I started fixing it up when I got back," Areon says, answering my thoughts. The little fort has been transformed. The roof is no longer sunk in, it has been replaced with new wood, with gutters that run along the sides of it. There are glass windows and potted plants and solar-powered fairy lights. It is everything I wanted as a child and more, a home away from home. I find it hard to believe that Areon did this.

"I can't believe you did all this," I say, running my fingers along the natural wooden walls.

"It wasn't too hard," he shrugs, "The hardest part was trying to remember how you wanted it to look."

"Well, you did a really good job." I take my phone out and turn the flashlight on, ducking inside the doorframe and into the middle of the room. Areon follows me inside, pulls out a lighter, and starts lighting candles.

"Setting the mood?" I joke. Areon smirks as the last candle catches the flame. Shadows crawl into the cracks of the wood, escaping from the candlelight.

"I'd ask what you want to know first, but I think it's better if I told you everything starting from the beginning." Areon stares into the flame of a candle.

"Okay," I stare at him, shadows dance around his face. He looks magical.

"Ten years ago, this is where we first met; only you didn't look like yourself. You were a—" he starts.

"A wolf, I know." I cut him off.

"And you thought I was some poor kid, someone who needed protection. It was the first time in my life that someone treated me as anything other than what I really was, *am.* I never wanted to leave, I wanted to stay here forever. But I couldn't. I don't belong in this world. I belong in the underworld with my parents. With Hades and Persephone. Areon isn't even my real name, its Zagreus." A cold breeze floats through the room, I shiver.

"Wait, like the Greek Gods Hades and Persephone?" I ask. "So that makes you... a God?" I have to force the word out of my mouth. Dad had only told me briefly of the Gods' existence, and now Areon is telling me that he *is* one? There is no way. This is too much.

"Yes. That is why when you found me here—well, when you found my corpse here—there was a drachma in my mouth. I have died and been brought back more times than I can count." Areon tells me.

"Can we backtrack a minute? You just dropped a huge bomb and you're just going to act like it was nothing?" I say.

"What do you mean?" Areon asks.

"I only found out that the Gods are real, like a few hours ago and now you're trying to tell me that you are one?"

"Yes, Rose. I'm telling you the truth."

"Then how did you die? I thought Gods were immortal." I ask.

"It was my time to return to the underworld, to return home. Hades pulled my spirit back to the underworld and I returned to my body later. My father often sends me here to hunt for him, I hunt down the spirits and the monsters that escape from the underworld." He shrugs like it's common knowledge.

"I'm sorry, what?" I say.

"It doesn't happen often, and it's not easy for them to do. But when they do escape, it's my job to capture them and bring them back to the underworld." He explains.

"So that's why you're here now?" I ask.

"Yes and no." He says.

"What do you mean?" I ask him. I need to know more.

"While Father likes the underworld and is well suited to rule it, he also enjoys making his brothers anxious. Inside my mother, there's a fire that burns for chaos and violence. They are the perfect match for one another. They start wars with the other Gods for fun and send me to find suitable warriors. The last time they did this, it was catastrophic to mankind and ended the lives of millions of people. Only in your history, it is known as the Black Death." Areon tells me.

"Wait, Hades started the Black Death?" I ask.

"Yes, it was his way of collecting warriors. They died, and he re-animated them, turning them into a species that wasn't dead nor alive but had the fighting power of a pack of lions." The candlelight shifts on his face, and I can't help but feel terrified of him for a moment.

"So, then why didn't we learn about that stuff in history?" I ask.

"Because Gods aren't allowed to interfere in the world anymore. It's the law, and humans can't know that we exist." He says.

"But why? Wouldn't it be easier?" I ask.

"In ways, yes. But long ago, there was a war between the Gods that lead to a stalemate between Ares and Zeus. It was either stop meddling in the human world or all of the gods would be killed, and Olympus would be no more, so Zeus agreed and sealed most of the doors to the earth. Although some of the other Gods would rather spend their time on earth than on Olympus." He tells me.

"Okay, so then why are you here going to school and hanging out in coffee shops?"

"When we were children, you always thought you were the protector, but I always looked out for you. I guess, part of me needed to know how you ended up. I kept an eye on you from a distance, and then I wanted to meet you to really get to know you. So, I enrolled in school and hung out at the coffee shop. I was rude at first, but only because I was afraid to get close to you and then have to leave again." He explains.

"So, you stalked me." I raise an eyebrow.

"What? No, I swear it wasn't like that." His eyes bug out, and he raises his hands in protest. I laugh and punch his leg.

"I'm kidding. I had to lighten the mood a little bit. You looked so serious, and it was giving me a headache." I laugh.

"I'm telling you the truth, Rose, how else would I look?" He says.

"I don't know. I just needed a break for a second." I say.

"I'm sorry, do you want me to take you home?" He asks.

"No, it's okay. I have more questions. This war that Hades is preparing, is it going to be as bad as the first one? I mean the Black Death killed close to twenty-five million people, are that many people going to die this time?" Areon sighs, and I lose him to his mind for a moment.

"I'm afraid that it'll be worse." He shifts his gaze to me, "These warriors he is having me collect weren't created by him, they are the product of Zeus and being trained as killing machines. I'm afraid that, this time, it might mean the end of the world."

"But why? Couldn't the other Gods stop it?" I ask.

"Most of them wouldn't care. A lot of the Gods despise humans. We're immortal for the most part. Only Ares has been strong enough to take any of the others out; especially Zeus." He explains.

"What about us? Could we stop them?" I blurt out.

Areon looks at me like he's Yoda, and I'm just some stupid kid without the force.

5

Everything Has Changed

Everything has changed. I curl up in my sheets and hug them against me. Nothing will ever be the same. I can't help but laugh at myself; I'm part wolf, Areon is a Greek God named Zagreus, Hades is plotting a war, and here I am, thinking that somehow, everything would stay the same. I mean, maybe between Andrew and me things will be semi-normal, but regarding everything else, there is no way. I hadn't told Andrew about everything that Areon and I had talked about. I would've overwhelmed him with everything, and I had only told him that I'm a wolf yesterday; it would've been way too much for him to handle. How am I supposed to tell him that there is a chance that everyone and everything he loves could die, including him?

I decide to avoid telling Andrew anything until at least lunchtime. There is no way to kill his mood when he's eating. Maybe by then, he'll be more prepared to hear it. I get dressed and head downstairs to find Deme has already left. Dad sits at the kitchen table, sipping coffee. I sit down across from him and sigh.

Can I tell him? Will he be able to handle it? I need to stop holding the past over him, maybe I can trust him.

"What's wrong, pumpkin?" he asks, looking over his newspaper.

"A lot," I say.

"You know if you're still feeling sore, you don't have to go to school today. I'll call you in." He says.

"It's not because of that. I actually don't feel sore anymore. It's everything else, the being a wolf and remembering everything, and the Greek Gods. There's so much going on that I don't know how to process everything." I say.

"You'll figure everything out. You're a smart girl. But if you want a little advice, mastering your transformation to the wolf is the most important." Dad tells me.

"Not when Hades is going to destroy the world," I mumble and hear a honk in the driveway. Andrew is here.

"What did you say?" Dad puts the newspaper down.

"Nothing, thanks for the chat, Dad. I got to go!" I said, getting up and heading out the door.

Andrew didn't ask any questions about what happened so far, and I am relieved for the normality before our world gets turned completely upside down. Gabby is hanging out with us though, which is probably why he didn't bring it up; there is no need to drag her in the middle of everything.

By the time lunch rolls around, I haven't seen Areon at all. He wasn't in the first hour, and I didn't run into him in the halls at all like we usually had. I was beginning to think that he might have run off before we could even say goodbye, but as Andrew and I sit down at our usual table, Areon pulls out a chair and sits down with us.

"Did you tell him yet?" Areon leans over and whispers in my ear. I shake my head, and Areon smiles, "Good." I look at him, puzzled. Why doesn't he want me to tell Andrew? Did he want to tell him everything himself? Before I get a chance to ask, Andrew has his own questions for Areon.

"So, Areon, why don't I remember you?" He blurts out, and Areon gives me a look before turning his attention back to Andrew.

"What are you talking about? We've only met." Areon states.

"Areon, I already told him that much," I say. Andrew stares at us, waiting for an answer.

Areon catches Andrew up with everything as we eat. Although, he leaves out the part about being a God himself, which I'm not sure why. Andrew stares at us for a few minutes after Areon finishes his story, his eyes darting back and forth between us like he is trying to figure out if we are pranking him. Finally, he relaxes and goes back to eating his sandwich.

"Alright then, what's the plan?" He asks.

"Excuse me?" Areon asks.

"What are we going to do about the whole Hades situation?" Andrew clarifies.

"We," Areon motions to each of us, "Aren't going to do anything, I, on the other hand, am going to find a way to stop him."

"Wait, what? You aren't going to let us help?" Andrew asks.

"Nope." He has no expression, and Andrew's face is showing every emotion I had when Areon told me that I couldn't help.

"Why not?" He asks

"Because you'll get yourselves killed. Here, you guys are safe." Areon tells him.

"If you think I'm going to let you go handle this by yourself, then you're insane," I state, and Andrew nods in agreement.

"I don't think, Rose, I *know* you are going to let me do this alone, because if you don't..." Areon trails off for a moment, "You could die, you both could. And what good would you be to your families then?" His gaze lingers on me for a little too long.

"What good would it be if all of us were dead?" Andrew says; I've never seen him so serious before. But he has a point, if Areon left and didn't succeed, then the world would be over, but if we went with him and help, he'd stand a better chance at being successful. Areon looks at me like he knows something that I don't.

"There is absolutely no way that you two are coming with me. End of discussion." Areon states. He stands up and leaves without another word.

I can't understand why Areon doesn't want us to help him, and without work to distract me, I can't get it out of my head. Instead of going home after school, Andrew and I drive out to where our old fort was. I wanted to show him what it looked like after all these years and see if he remembers it.

"We need to come up with a plan," Andrew states as we turn down the dirt road that leads to the fort.

"A plan for what?" I ask him.

"To make sure that Areon doesn't leave without us." He answers.

"You saw his face. There is no way that he is going to let us go with him," I tell him.

"That's why we find out when he's leaving, and we follow him," Andrew says.

"What if he whips up a portal and disappears with it. Neither of us knows how to get to the underworld or wherever it would take him." I say, and he thinks it over for a moment.

"Wait, so portals exist too? What is Areon, some kind of magician? If he does, then we just jump in after him." Andrew laughs, and I realize that I've basically just spilled the God secret.

"Okay, agreed. I think he's more likely to tell me when he's leaving, though, so I'll be the one to get it out of him when he's leaving." I say, Andrew nods.

IN THE SHADOWS | 99

When we arrive at the fort, Andrew looks around for a while at all the new additions, like I had. He can't believe that he had forgotten it.

"Do you think anyone else has ever stumbled upon it?" He asks.

"No, I don't think so. It's pretty far away from any houses." I guess.

"Yeah, you're probably right." He says.

"So, you remember it?" I question him.

"Yeah, I mean, I always remembered us being out here, but I guess, when I lost my memory of Areon, all of these memories got blurred out. Speaking of which, did he ever say why I couldn't remember him?"

"Because I forced you to forget," Areon states, making both Andrew and I jump. I didn't even hear him pull up, let alone hear his footsteps as he walked towards us.

"What do you mean forced me?" Andrew rolls his eyes.

"When I told you that Hades was planning on attacking mankind, I left something out. But I didn't want to tell you in front of everyone at school, so I waited." Areon says, making his way closer to us.

"Cryptic. But okay, tell me then. You're a wizard, aren't you?" Andrew says, then he leans against the fort, amused.

"My real name is Zagreus, and I am the son of Hades." Areon states, and Andrew laughs.

"No, really. What didn't you tell me?" Andrew asks, still smiling, and Areon and I look at each other.

"I told you." Areon raises an eyebrow, "How else would I know that Hades was planning a war?"

"Oh. Yeah, I guess I skipped over that fact, didn't I?" Andrew looks at me and shrugs. "Well, what other information am I missing then? What else aren't you telling me?" He asks. I am curious as to how Areon is going to answer because, at this point, I am sure that we are all caught up on everything.

"That's it," Areon says flatly, I don't believe him.

"How come you can tell us about you, that you're a God and the son of Hades? I thought that because of the rules, humans weren't allowed to know that you existed?" I ask Areon.

"Because, Rose, you are technically a creation of Zeus and shouldn't exist either. Telling you doesn't count. Andrew, on the other hand, I can wipe his memory again when I need to." He answers.

"Hey! That's not fair!" Andrew yells.

"I'm not going to, just don't tell anyone else about me. Otherwise, we would all be in trouble. And Ares is the last God we need snooping around here." Areon says.

"Guess I should delete that Facebook post then," Andrew says, pulling out his phone. Areon and I both go wide-eyed and lunge for the phone, "Kidding." Andrew laughs, pulling the phone out of our reach.

Areon offers to take me home when he realizes how tired Andrew is getting. Although before he heads out, Andrew pulls me to the side and tells me to let him know when Areon leaves my house so we can follow him and be sure that he doesn't leave without us. As soon as Andrew's truck is out of sight, Areon relaxes.

"Why don't you like Andrew?" I ask him.

"What do you mean?" Areon asks.

"I mean that, whenever he's around, you get all tense and you seem annoyed. If we were all so close as children, then why don't you treat him like we were?" I clarify.

"It's not that I don't like him, it is more that I find him annoying. He's a normal human, he doesn't know what it means to be a part of something bigger." Areon explains, sitting down next to me.

"But I'm a human, and you don't treat me like that." I point out.

"You're not a normal human, though. You're part wolf. That makes you different. Plus, have you ever seen that kid eat? It's disgusting." He laughs

"He's… eccentric. He really is different than most people. Maybe you need to get to know him better." I offer.

"Yeah, maybe." He replies.

"Is everything okay?" I ask, Areon meets my eyes.

"How did you know that you were part wolf before I told you? I mean, you led on like you had no idea, and I know that your memory went away. So how did you know?" He asks me.

"I saw something that triggered my memories to return, and when that happened, I turned. It was almost simultaneously." I pull out my phone and scroll through the pictures on it, "This is what triggered them." I show Areon the picture of us as children, and he stares at it, wide-eyed.

"That's not possible." He states, "I erased everyone's memory of me. I was thorough about it too. This picture shouldn't exist." He tells me.

"But it does, I found it in an old yearbook from when we were in elementary school," I explain.

"Wait, they make yearbooks for elementary schools?" He asks.

I laugh, "Apparently."

"That explains it then." He rolls his eyes.

"Can I ask you something?" I ask, and Areon nods, "When are you leaving?"

"Soon. I've already been here for almost two weeks." He answers.

"Two weeks? But you've only been in school for like three days!" I exclaim, "We just got you back."

"I told you, I watched you for a while before I wanted to actually decide to hang out with you. If I don't go back, they'll think something is wrong, and I already told you once—"

"Gods can't meddle in human affairs." We say in unison, and Areon looks at me with shock.

"You've only said it a million times already." I nag.

"Rose, I'm sorry. But I promise that I will say goodbye before I go." He says, wrapping me in a big hug. He holds me tightly for longer than he should have, but I don't mind. I relax into him, embracing the smell of teakwood on his clothes. I'm not sure why I feel this way, but I know that he is lying. He is leaving tonight.

I call Andrew when I get home, but it goes straight to voicemail. Instead of calling him again, I go to find my dad. He is in the living room when I find him, watching something on the history channel; something we used to do together when I was a kid. I sit down next to him, and he smiles at me. I'm proud of him, I didn't think that he would change. I thought that he was going to be my drunk, uncaring dad for the rest of my life. But here he is, proving me wrong.

"Dad," I start, "If one day, I didn't come home..." I pause, I can see the panic in his eyes, "I don't want you to think it's because I ran away," I add, thinking of Phoenix, "I would never do that. But if I did, I don't want you to worry. Okay?"

"Rose, you're my daughter. I will be worried about you for the rest of my life. What's going on, though?" He inquires, its enough to bring tears to my eyes.

"I need to go do something; I need to make sure the world is safe. I can't tell you more than that, I just need you to trust me, and I need you to make sure that Deme is okay when I'm gone." I say. I should just tell him the truth, he used to be a wolf too. But I can't.

"Rose, you're freaking me out." He says, he mutes the tv so he can place all of his attention on me.

"I know, but it's the only way. I need to leave to protect you, but I promise I'll be back. Just don't leave her. You can't check out of her life again, it'll destroy her." I didn't realize that saying this would be that hard, but I needed to tell him. I couldn't leave him and Deme without warning because I don't want him to relapse and turn to drinking again. He already lost one kid; he won't survive losing another.

"What are you going to say to Deme?" He questions.

"I can't say goodbye to her, she'll know that I'm lying. I need you to tell her that I'm going to Grandma's for the week or something. She'll still be able to call and text. I can't lie to her face." I frown.

Dad is reluctant to let me go, but I need to pack a bag, and I've already told him enough. Upstairs, I call Andrew again.

"Rose? It's so late. What's wrong?" He answers groggily. Obviously, he has forgotten our arrangement.

"Areon's leaving tonight. Get dressed and pack a bag. I'll meet you at the end of the street in ten minutes." I tell him.

"Wait, how do you know he's leaving tonight?" He questions.

"I just know. I could see it in his eyes when we were talking. He's leaving." I tell him.

"Okay, I'm up. I'll see you then." Andrew hangs up, and I start packing a bag. I am not sure how long we will be gone, so I pack most of my clothes, which isn't enough to even fill two backpacks. I shove a jar filled with all of the tips I've made working at common grounds in between my clothes to protect it. Who knows how long we'll be gone? I leave a note in my vanity drawer that tells my bank information just in case something bad happens, so Deme can have access to it if she needs it. I doubt there are ATMs in the underworld anyway.

Andrew picks me up exactly ten-minutes later, and we head straight to Areon's house. It was difficult trying to remember where he lived considering it was night, I had only been there once, and I only remembered how to leave his house. When we're about a mile away from Areon's house, Andrew turns off his lights and parks in some bushes. It is time to walk.

"Do you think he heard us coming?" Andrew asks, handing me my backpack from his truck bed.

"I don't know. Hopefully, he hasn't left yet, though," I say. We walk the rest of the way to Areon's house in silence, mostly so we could listen for his car coming.

Luckily, we get to Areon's house before he left. As quietly as we can, Andrew and I open Areon's jeep and climb into the trunk to hide. It's a tight space for both of us to fit into, especially with our bags on top of us. We wait for about fifteen minutes before we hear Areon heading to the car. Unfortunately, he finds us almost instantly.

"No." Areon states, opening the trunk. "Absolutely not."

"It always works in the movies. "Andrew shrugs.

"Well, this isn't a movie." Areon isn't amused, "Now go home."

"No, we're coming with you. Whether you like it or not." I insist, folding my arms. Areon makes serious eye contact with me. He is challenging me, trying to figure out if he can make me leave or not. "Even if you leave us here, we will find a way to follow you. We aren't going to let you do this alone." I say, and Areon sighs—I win.

"Listen, you guys know that you're risking your lives, right? Once we leave, there is no turning back." Areon's voice is quiet, but stern and, for a split second, I can't help but want to go home. I'd finally gotten everything I wanted, Dad is sober and taking care of us again, I have my memories back, and I don't have to take care of everything anymore; I could finally be a kid again. But if I don't help or at least try to help, then I am risking more than my life, I am risking everyone's. I think back to what Dr. Foster had said to me: *Go home, Finish school, fall in love. Live your life,* he'd said. So how am I supposed to do all of that if there is no life left? I look at Andrew and then back at Areon.

"I'm coming," I tell him.

We drive for hours in the pitch black of night. Andrew had fallen asleep in the backseat almost instantly; I swear he can fall asleep anywhere. I sit next to Areon in the front seat. He hasn't said much since we left, I can't tell if he's mad that we are coming with him or happy. I don't really care much, either way. We need to do this, *I* need to do this. We just need to drive to California to some crater that holds the entrance to the underworld, and we'll adjust the plan from there. It is a six-and-a-half-hour drive to the crater. We should be getting there around midnight, depending on how traffic is.

"You should try to get some sleep." Areon whispers.

"I'll be fine." I smile at him, but he isn't buying it.

"No," he shakes his head. "You'll need your rest." I haven't slept in almost twenty-four hours, but I don't want him to accidentally fall asleep while driving, and the best way to keep him awake is for me to stay awake too.

"I couldn't sleep if I wanted to," I state.

"Why? Is something wrong? Is it too hot or cold? Do you need anything?" Areon panics, adjusting the air conditioning back and forth.

"No, I'm okay. I can't sleep in cars, that's all." I laugh, and he relaxes again.

"Gabby," Andrew mutters in his sleep. Areon and I look at each other and burst out into laughter, I try to stay quiet for Andrew's sake, but he wakes up anyway.

"What!" He sits up and pops his head between Areon and me in the front seat. "What did I miss?" He questions, which makes us laugh harder. It's the first time I hear Areon genuinely laugh, and for a split second, I think that it might be the only time I will ever hear him laugh again, but I can't think like that. I push any negative thoughts out of my head and savor the moment.

"So what's the plan again?" I ask Areon.

"Well, since you two are with me," He gestures to Andrew and me, "We'll need to go to one of the entrances to the underworld. The closest is in California, a place called the Amboy Crater."

"I can't believe the entrance to the underworld is so close." Andrew says, he's looking out the window now.

"There are many of them all around the world, hundreds actually. Although most are unusable now. The easiest to get to are the ones located in what you call craters." Areon goes on explaining that because forest thinning and more cities being built that most of the entrances have been covered or destroyed. I'm having trouble listening to him though, keeping my eyes open has become a chore.

I'm not sure how long I've been asleep, but I wake up to the sound of an alarm screaming at me.

"Shit," Areon says under his breath. He pushes a bunch of buttons on the center console. "No," He says louder, "No way. Not Now."

"What's going on?" I ask, sitting up and looking at the GPS. It looks like a radar, like the kind you'd see in movies, with a single dot in the center and a red dot blinking farther away from the other.

"I'm sorry, I didn't mean to wake you." The alarm stops, but the red dot stays. I'm not sure what I'm looking at, but I know it can't be good.

"Damn it." Areon sighs, pushes a button on the console, and turns onto the next available road.

"Where are we going?" I ask him. The road gets progressively bumpier as we drive down it.

"There's something I've got to take care of." He answers me. We drive down the road for a while before I finally spot a road sign that states where we were headed: ARIS ZOO. Why are we going to a zoo? Is this a joke? I don't understand, and Andrew doesn't either.

"Are we going to a zoo?" Andrew asks groggily. I didn't realize that he had woken up.

"No, I'm going to the Zoo. You two," Areon motions to Andrew and me. "Are going to stay in the car." He says.

"Why, what's going on?" I ask.

"Remember when I told you that it's my job to hunt down the monsters that escape the underworld?" Areon asks.

"No way! That's awesome!" Andrew exclaims.

"Yeah, I remember," I answer.

"Well, something is here, and I need to get it back where it belongs," Areon tells us. Areon drives straight up to the entrance of the Zoo, ignoring all the parking spots and hopping the curb to get here. The building looks like it belongs some apocalyptic television show. All of the animal statues are covered in ivy and moss. The building zoo has clearly been abandoned for a long time. Graffiti is on most of the walls and even on the pathways.

"You've got to be kidding me." Areon sighs, pulling his seatbelt off. We aren't the only ones here. A row of motorcycles, one after the other, sits in front of a giant statue of an elephant that is overgrown with ivy.

"Listen to me very closely; you and Andrew have to stay here. No matter what you hear or see. You guys cannot follow me." Areon states in a hushed tone.

"Why? We are here to help you remember?" Andrew folds his arms, pouting.

"Because if you don't, we'll have a lot more to worry about than the God of death." Areon threatens.

"What do you mean? Who's here?" I ask.

"One of my crazy cousins. Please take my word for it." Areon explains. I nod in response, "Do you guys promise you'll stay here?" He adds, I look at Andrew, who is still pouting in the backseat.

"I'll do my best to make sure he stays here," I answer, Areon nods. He gets out of the car and disappears into the shadows.

"You're not really about to let him go alone, are you?" Andrew asks me.

"Yes, he does this for a living. He'll be fine." I don't want to leave him alone. I want to help him, but if he gets caught with Andrew, he'll be accused of breaking the treaty or whatever they call it. The last thing I want is for Areon to be killed because of us.

"You know, with all of these vines, we could probably climb up to the roof and watch," Andrew smirks. I look around outside and see that he is right. There are thick vines everywhere, and if we climbed to the top of the elephant statue, we could easily get to the top of the roof. Andrew smiles and lifts his eyebrows repeatedly, his own version of the puppy dog face. I want to listen to Areon and stay put, but I also wanted to see him at work.

"Fine, but we have to be quiet." I finally decide.

"Yes!" Andrew yells, I cover his mouth and put my finger to my lips.

"I said quiet." I tell him. We sneak out of the jeep, careful not to slam the doors shut behind us and start climbing up the elephant. I am faster at climbing up than Andrew, which I accredit to my wolf half; even though he was never athletic, to begin with.

It takes us five minutes to find Areon. He is surprisingly good at hiding in the shadows, which I guess makes sense, given that he does this for a living. We skulk around the rooftops trying to get a better view when I hear another set of footsteps and freeze.

"Zagreus!" A deep voice calls out, "I was wondering when you'd show up." I quietly scan the area, looking for anyone other than Areon. Finally, a group of bikers walks out of one of the other buildings. Six bikers in total; five men and one woman.

"What's going on?" Andrew leans over to me and whispers.

"We need to get closer." I shrug. We tiptoe across the roof to get a better view, and find a spot covered in shadow to hide in as we watch.

"Ares, I should've known you'd be here," Areon smirks, and I freeze again. Ares was single-handedly responsible for the Gods' rule against intervening in human affairs. If he catches Andrew and me, Areon will be screwed. I get better eyes on the bikers. It is now obvious that two of them are Gods, and the rest are normal humans; I guess Ares doesn't have to follow his own rules. Ares is double the size of the other men, especially in muscle size. They basically bulge out from under his black t-shirt; I'm surprised the sleeves haven't torn. The woman has legs for days and gorgeous blonde hair that shines when it moves. I have no doubt in my mind that she is Aphrodite.

"Long time no see, Aphrodite, how's your husband?" Areon calls out to her. The look she gives him could kill.

"You smell like a dog, doing any recruiting lately?" she hisses, and I feel a pit in my stomach. I don't know what she meant by 'recruiting,' but I could tell it bothered Areon, he shifts his balance between each leg. Ares looks back and forth between the two and looks around.

"No, that's not him. There's a wolf here somewhere." Ares scans the area. Areon's eyes dart up to where I am. I step back, hiding myself further into the shadows. I know Areon is a hunter, but I am the last thing he needs to worry about.

"Come out, come out wherever you are, wolf," Ares shouts, "Don't make us force you out of hiding, we're on your side." Even if he is telling the truth, I don't believe him.

"Well, if you're not going to show yourself, then I guess I'm going to have to force you out of hiding." Ares sneers, grabs Areon, and restrains his arms. Areon doesn't even struggle, he holds perfectly still. "Aphrodite, would you release our little friend," Ares smirks.

"I'm not one of your henchmen," she sneers, "But seeing as I would like to see this through, I'll go fetch it for you." she walks into the darkness, the only inkling I have as to where she is, is the sound of her heels clicking on the asphalt. The wait is agony, not knowing what is going on, or if Areon can get himself out of this mess, kills me.

A growl.

A low, deep, menacing growl. I can't see anything, but I know that whatever "friend" Aphrodite went to get is huge. Silently, a creature creeps out of the shadows. It is unlike anything I have ever seen before. A lion, with the head of a goat on its back and the tail of a snake. It skulks out into the light and walks circles around Ares and Areon. The hair on my neck stands tall.

"Meet my Chimera. I found him here, feeding on the other animals when they shut this place down." Ares grins.

"You think a wolf is going to come anywhere near that thing? You really must not know anything about wolves." Areon laughs. He's right. Every bone in my body screams at me to run, to pick a direction, and never come back. But I can't leave Areon, not until I know he is safe.

"Andrew," I whisper, "you need to go back to the car as quietly as possible, lock the doors, and if anyone that isn't Areon or me approaches the car, I want you to drive away." Andrew nods in response; every ounce of color has drained from his body. I help him climb over a ledge before he slips away into the darkness.

I turn my attention back to Areon, Ares is tying his hands behind his back while the Chimera continues to circle them. I have no view of Aphrodite or the other henchmen if they're even still here. I'm downwind, and I can't smell them.

"Well then, now that you're all tied up and can't do anything to save yourself from being ripped apart by this Chimera, I'll hope your friend comes to save you and be on my way." Ares starts to walk away. Areon makes no attempt at trying to free himself. He is calmer than anyone else in this situation would be.

"Hades won't let you get away with this!" Areon calls out, Ares laughs in response and disappears into the shadows. I watch the Chimera as it continues to circle Areon, planning its move. It stops and smells the ground. Any minute now, it will make its move and rip Areon to pieces. The snake tail hisses with excitement. I am sure the beast hasn't eaten in days.

I take a deep breath. It's now or never. I am either going to jump off the roof and land as a wolf, or I am going to have to roll when I land, so I don't shatter my ankles. Thankfully, I perform a combination of the two. I leap from the top of the rooftop without thinking too hard about it. As I fall, my bones shift, and my spine curls. Dad was right, the transformation is less painful the more I do it. Although I still need to fight back from screaming as my bones slide into place. When I hit the ground, I have barely finished changing and land on my side. Areon's expression shifts from panic to shock, and finally to anger when he realizes it is me.

"I told you to stay put. You promised!" He yells at me, struggling with the rope at his wrists.

"A female? Wow, I wasn't expecting this! "Ares' voice booms from the zoo speakers. Areon's eyes dart around, searching for Ares.

"Ares! Stop this!" He pleads, but there is only silence. I attempt to move towards Areon, but the Chimera blocks my path and growls. Every step I take, the Chimera matches me. I dodge around it and sprint over to Areon, but before I can reach him, the Chimera knocks me down from the side. I bite at its paws as it swipes at me, but the snakehead is faster than me and bites into my skin. I howl in pain, kicking the Chimera from me. I'm not sure what the goat head has in store for me, but the claws and fangs have already done too much damage. I lunge at the beast, sinking my own teeth into its neck and shake violently. I've never fought as a wolf, but my instincts are making up for it. The beast throws me again, this time closer to Areon, and I manage to cut through part of his rope with my teeth before the monster tackles me again. This time, it's damaging, the snake bites into me more times than I can count, and the lion head desperately reaches to get at my neck. I get thrown into the air before I can react. A rib breaks on impact, and I can feel the blood spilling from under my black fur.

"Rose!" Areon yells in terror as he rips the rope off his wrists. I try but fail to get up as the Chimera inches its way to me, readying itself for a final blow. I start to black out. My vision blurs. All I can make out is the figure of the beast. I curl into myself, bracing for impact when I realize I am human again, if the Chimera hits me again, I'll be dead.

The ground shakes.

I squint, trying to see what is happening when the earth splits under the Chimera's feet, and a bright white light emerges from the hole. My hands drip with blood, it takes everything in me, but with one final push, I call out for Areon before I fade into nothing.

6

Room 93

The room I wake up in is dark, aside from the blue glow from the muted television. The air conditioning is on so high, I am sure you can see my breath. I stare at the blue screen on the television and feel like I am dreaming. As my eyes adjust to the strange light, I can make out another bed, although it remains untouched and made perfectly. The hotel room is fairly similar to every hotel that I've ever been in; it even smells the same. I am distracted from looking around the room by a rustling on the other side of the door, followed by a click and a beep. The door opens and reveals Andrew, who is tiptoeing into the room.

"Oh, you're awake!" He shouts when he is sure that my eyes were open. He makes his way over to the bed and sits at the edge, dumping a handful of packaged food next to us.

"How long have I been asleep?" I ask him. I attempt to sit up, but a sharp pain in my ribs sends me back down.

"About four months," Andrew tells me, ripping open a bag of Doritos.

"What!" I yell.

"Calm down, I'm kidding. It's only been four days." He says, rubbing his ear.

"Four days is still a long time, Andrew, what happened? Where's Areon? Did Ares see you? What happened to the Chimera? How's—" I get cut off by Andrew.

"Woah there, pony-boy, one question at a time." He laughs and pulls out his phone and begins typing. "Areon will be here in a minute, and everything is okay." He tells me.

"What happened, though?" I ask.

"I'm not sure, I went back to the car, and there was an earthquake, and this bright white light, and then there was nothing. Silence. It was hard to sit there and wait, but when I was about to go look for you guys, Areon came walking up, carrying you in his arms. Then, we drove to this random hotel, and you've been asleep since." He explains.

"Why haven't I healed yet then? I still feel like I've been hit by a semi-truck," I ask.

"You fought a Chimera, Rose." Areon states, but I didn't even hear him come in. "You broke numerous ribs, your wrist, and your foot, plus we had to re-break a few bones because they healed too fast and wrong. We didn't expect you to wake up for at least another week." He says, pulls the armchair in the room next to my bedside, and sits down. Andrew shoves a few chips into his mouth before he stands up.

"Well, I'm starving, and continental breakfast ends in thirty minutes. So, I'll be back with some real food, and we can catch up." Andrew pats my leg and waves before leaving the room.

"So, what happened to the Chimera?" I ask Areon.

"I sent it back to the Underworld." He answers.

"How?" I ask.

"What do you mean *how*? It's my job. I open up a portal, catch whatever I need to and send it back to Hades. That's how it works." He explains.

"Then, how come we can't use the same portal to get to the underworld instead of road-tripping across two states?" I ask him. He shifts his weight in the chair.

"I've never used the portal on a human, and I don't know if Andrew would survive it." He tells me.

"But you can?" It's a dumb question, I realize this the second it comes out of my mouth.

"I'm a God, Rose. I'm immortal." He rolls his eyes. "But since we're on that subject now, I want you and Andrew to go home. "

"What? No!" I protest.

"It's too dangerous, and I can't let you get hurt again, either of you." Areon's eyes are pleading with me to obey.

"No way, I'm not going back. And I thought you didn't even like Andrew." I cross my arms.

"I've been sharing a room with him for four days, what was I supposed to do? Ignore him? Listen, you are hurt, and he is a human. If he were the one attacked by the chimera, he would be dead right now, and this all would have been for nothing." He explains to me as if I don't already know.

"I'm fine, okay. I can't give up now, not after how far we've come!" I tell him.

"Rose, you were attacked and almost killed by a Chimera!" Areon yells.

"Well, I lived, didn't I?" I know that Areon is right, my guts say that I should've gone home days ago. I won't leave now, though. Areon stands up and paces the length of the room. I lift myself up the best I can and relax against the headboard. I can't tell what he is thinking, but for five minutes straight, he paces the room until finally, he sits next to me on the bed.

"Rose, can't you see that I'm trying to protect you?" He says.

"I can protect myself," I state.

"Yeah, because that worked *so* well last time." Areon mumbles.

"Excuse me?" I fire back, and he buries his head in his hands.

"I... I can't lose you. Not again." He says, peeking out behind his fingers.

"I'm still here, Areon. You didn't lose anyone. Andrew and I are still alive, and we aren't going to leave you." I tell him.

"You don't get it," He buries his face in his hands again, "You are the only good thing in my never-ending existence. You don't see me as a God or the son of Hades, you see me for me." He looks up at me again, "I can't lose that." He says, and I lose all of my words. I almost feel guilty for coming here, for putting my life in danger, but I can't pack up and go home now. I stare into his eyes, searching for the words to say, but there aren't any.

Areon's breathing is heavy, and his eyes stay locked onto mine as he inches forward and caresses my cheeks. He kisses me. Slow and steady at first, then all at once, we are wrapped in each other's embrace. It is at this moment that I know I need him. I will do anything for him.

Areon pulls away from me too soon. I'm too distracted to hear the beep and click of the door opening. He jumps away from the bed and stands at the wall just as Andrew enters the room.

"You guys won't believe how much food they had out! "Andrew says, dropping an assortment of fruits and packaged pastries onto the bed.

"Let me guess. This is only a quarter of the amount you brought back too." Areon jokes. He's breathing heavily.

"No, I tried to bring more, but they wouldn't let me." Andrew starts digging in his pockets, "They didn't, however, check my pockets before I left." He smiles triumphantly, and I can't help but laugh.

"Is there any for us, or is all that for you?" I joke, and Andrew shoots me a look.

"I got you an apple." He says, handing it to me, "Anyway, what's the plan now that Rose is awake? Are we going to go after Hades now?" Areon's face straightens out. He still wants us to go home.

"Areon wants us to go home," I say. My heart is still racing.

"Oh, I know. He's been trying to convince me to leave since we got here, but now that you're better, we can stay, right?" Andrew asks Areon before biting into a cinnamon roll.

"You are both the most stubborn people I know. Rose can't even walk yet." Areon says.

"I can walk!" I fight back, Areon rolls his eyes at me and sighs.

"Fine," He says. "We'll leave tomorrow."

"What's the plan, though? Or are we going to wing it?" Andrew asks.

"Well, the closest entry point to the underworld is still a couple hours' drive from here. We'll head there and hope that no one is waiting for us." Areon states, sitting down on the armchair next to the bed again, I get goosebumps.

"Great plan," Andrew says sarcastically.

"Who would be waiting for us?" I ask.

"I don't know, Ares again. But probably not. The entry is at the bottom of the crater, and some cult goes there to worship Satan or something, so maybe them?" Areon says.

"I'm sorry, did you say Satan worshippers?" I ask.

"I know, right? What kind of name is Satan?" Areon chuckles. Andrew and I look at each other, both of us unsure if Areon is being serious. We wait awkwardly for him to say something else, but he doesn't.

"Anyway," I start, "is there a pool here? I'd love to get some pressure off my bones and float for a while."

Areon doesn't join Andrew and me at the pool. Instead, he sits in his room doing who knows what. I want to talk to him. About the chimera, about what we're doing, about the kiss. It takes everything I have not to think about it, but as soon as there is any silence, it drifts back into my mind. Why did he do it? I'm glad he did, but I never thought it would happen. He had so many better opportunities to kiss me, why not do it then? Was he just using the kiss as a way of making me want to go back home? If so, his plan definitely backfired.

"Have you talked to Gabby at all?" I ask Andrew. We lie on some towels next to the pool.

"Every chance I can." He beams at me.

"Yeah? so things are going well then?" I welcome the normal conversation; it feels like ages since we talked about home.

"Yeah, things are great! She's amazing." He blushes.

"What does she think you're doing out here?" I ask.

"I told her that I was visiting my dad since he's stationed out here." He tells me.

"And what does your mom think?" I ask him, turning over on the towel.

"She thinks I'm at home. She's actually still visiting my dad right now." He explains.

'Oh, well, that works out perfect then." I say.

'Yeah." He sighs, I can tell he misses home.

"What happened that night? At the party, I mean, did you guys hook up?" I ask him.

"What? No!" Andrew panics, "We talked all night. We actually walked away into the woods and laid out under the stars; it was super easy to talk to her once we got away from everyone. I don't know, it feels like we were made for each other." He smiles from ear to ear, and his eyes light up in a way I've never seen. "What about you?" He asks.

"What about me?" I ask.

"What happened to you at the party? You never told me." He clarifies. *Oh, me? I got drunk and almost got raped by Tyler, no big deal.* There is no way I can tell him that.

"Nothing important, I got really drunk, and Areon tried to take me home, but I fell asleep before I could tell him where to go so, I ended up staying the night at his house," I tell him instead.

"Wait, you stayed at his place?" Andrew raises his eyebrows.

"Yeah."

"Did you guys hook up?" Andrew is wide-eyed.

"No, he slept on the couch," I tell him.

"Oh." He looks at the ground.

"Don't sound too disappointed." I joke.

"What? I'm not." He defends himself.

"Sure you're not." I roll my eyes and turn back over.

"Well, I don't know. Maybe I am. I think you'd be good together." He tells me, and I have to hide my face from blushing.

"Even though he's a God?" I ask.

"Yeah, I mean, I kind of keep forgetting about that." He sighs.

"We're literally on our way to the underworld to try to convince Hades that he shouldn't try to end the world, and you keep forgetting that Areon is a God?" I say.

"Well, when you put it that way, I sound pretty stupid." He looks down again.

"Sorry." I apologize.

"It's okay. I got a lot going on in this thick skull of mine." He tells me.

"I'm sorry. Did you want to go home? Areon would be pretty stoked if we went back now." I ask although I hope he says no.

"No, this is actually the best thing going on right now in my life; well, besides Gabby. This trip is so fun in so many ways, I almost feel like a kid again. Areon gave me back the memories of all of us when you were asleep, and I feel so great full for this whole experience."

"He gave you back your memories?" I ask.

"Yeah, it was really weird at first, but he has the power to take and give back memories, that's why we didn't remember him." He explains.

"So, you remember everything now?" I ask.

"I mean, I never really forgot. I forgot Areon, like he took himself out of my memories or buried them so deep it was like he didn't exist." He tells me.

"So, he erased himself from everyone's memories?" I ask

"I guess so. I don't really know how it works." Andrew shrugs, "Are you hungry? I'll go get us some take-out if you want."

"Sure." I'm not hungry, but he always is.

"Alright, I'm going to head back to my room and change first, did you want to come with?" He asks me, standing up and rolling up his towel.

"No, I'm alright here," I tell him.

"Alright, I'll be back in a bit then." Andrew disappears behind the pool fence.

The sun starts to set, and my skin is pruned up from the amount of time I've spent in the water. I don't want to go back to the hotel room yet, so I lie on one of the pool chairs and watch as the sun drifts down below the horizon.

"Can I sit here?" Areon's voice asks from behind me, I nod. We haven't been alone since this morning when he kissed me, and I still don't know what to say to him. "Where'd Andrew go?" He asks.

"He went to go get us food; you didn't see him on his way out?" I ask.

"No, I guess we missed each other." Areon shrugs

"What did you do all day?" I ask him.

"Oh, I made sure that the Chimera made it back to where it belongs."

"And did it?"

"Yeah, we don't have to worry about that one anymore." I can't help but feel like he was as nervous about talking to me as I am him. "So, I'm sorry about earlier." He says.

"What?"

"I'm sorry that I... I'm sorry that I did that earlier without asking for your permission first." He tries to clarify, but I still don't know what he is talking about.

"What are you talking about?" I ask.

"When I kissed you earlier. I shouldn't have done so without asking first." He blushes.

"You... You don't have to ask for permission for that." I stutter.

"I was raised in a different world than you were. I could be punished severely for that back home." He looks down at the pool, "Plus, after what happened with Tyler, I don't want to hurt you."

"You could never hurt me," I tell him.

"That's what you think." He mumbles under his breath, but I choose to ignore it.

"So, why'd you do it then? "I ask.

"Do what?"

"Kiss me, why did you kiss me then?"

"Because I had to." He says.

"What do you mean you had to?"

"I had to know. I needed you to know how much you mean to me." He says. I don't know how to respond to him.

"Rose, Areon, did you guys hear what happened? "Andrew asks from behind us, and I almost jump out of my skin.

"No, what's going on?" Areon stands, ready to spring into action as if someone is going to burst through the door and attack us.

"Tyler was escorted out of school this morning by the police. Apparently, he tried to sleep with a girl that was passed out drunk at that party we went to." Andrew says. A cold chill runs through my body. Areon quickly shoots me a look. "Wait, what's going on?" Andrew asks. I should've told him sooner. I should have said something to someone, maybe then, Tyler wouldn't have tried again. "Seriously, someone tell me what's going on," Andrew says desperately.

I spend the next half hour explaining to Andrew what had happened the night of the party. Areon fills in the parts that I missed, and how he walked up on what was happening. Andrew is quiet throughout the whole story. Occasionally, he nods his head to let us know that he is still listening. For a while, all he can say is how sorry he is.

"Rose." Andrew whispers, "I'm so sorry that happened to you."

"It's fine, Andrew. I was the one who went out by myself." I tell him.

"Yeah, but... if I had been there, he wouldn't have even tried to do that. If I hadn't been so caught up with Gabby, you wouldn't have left. You didn't even want to go to the party. It's all my fault." Andrew buries his face in his hands.

"Andrew, there is no possible way that you could have known what was going to happen. And nothing did happen, I'm fine." I explain, "Please don't blame yourself."

"How do I not?" I look up from his hands, and his eyes are red.

"Seriously, dude, don't beat yourself up. I stopped him, Rose is okay, and Tyler will be in jail for a long time." Areon chimes in, and I am grateful that he does, I didn't know if he was still upset that I'd wanted to tell Andrew about it that night or not.

"Honestly, I think if it hadn't happened, I never would have been able to turn into a wolf again," I state, and both boys look at me, confused.

"What?" Areon asks, raising an eyebrow.

"When Tyler had me pinned down, I felt like my back was breaking. I think that was my body trying to turn, only I haven't done it since I was a kid so I couldn't. I think somewhere deep down, I knew I could do it though, so as a fight or flight response, I tried to change, but I couldn't." I explain to them.

"You need to report your experience to the police," Andrew states out of nowhere.

"No, she doesn't," Areon says. The two of them glare at each other.

"It's my decision what I do and when I do it, neither of you gets a say," I tell them, their expressions soften. Andrew apologizes.

"Of course, you do, that's all I was trying to say," Areon says.

We decide to go back to our rooms, Andrew and Areon are in room ninety-five, I'm in the adjoining room number ninety-three. They both leave me alone to pack my things, although there isn't much to pack since I've been sleeping the entire time we've been here. I decide on taking a shower before we head out onto the road again. The chlorine from the pool still sits on my skin, and who knows when the next time I'll be able to shower is.

We're back on the road in less than an hour. Areon said we only have a few more hours until we get to the entrance of the underworld, and we should try to get some rest in the car before we get there, but I don't think I could sleep another minute if I wanted to. I cannot believe everything we had been through on this trip so far. I feel closer to Andrew than I ever have, and I don't know what's going to happen to Areon after all of this, but I don't want to lose him again.

I check the back seat to see if Andrew has fallen asleep, and he has. I could tell he felt guilty about what happened that night at the party, but I assured him that it wasn't his fault, and Areon did too.

"Thank you for giving Andrew his memories back," I said to Areon.

"He deserved to get them back."

"Yeah." I stare out the window, watching the blur of the desert pass by us. "Did you take mine too?" I finally ask after a few minutes.

"I tried." He states.

"What do you mean tried?"

"Well, I was a kid. My ability to alter memories wasn't as strong as it was when I was in the underworld. You wouldn't let me, you fought it harder than anyone else had, and that's why you lost all of your memories." He explains.

"Wait, so you're the reason why?" I ask

"Yeah, sorry about that, by the way." He smirks.

"So, you gave them back then?"

"No, you got them back on your own. I had nothing to do with it." He shrugs.

I pull out my phone and scroll through my social media. Someone had posted a video of Tyler being pulled out of school. He didn't even look sorry for what he had done, and it makes me sick.

"What's wrong?" Areon asks, looking over at me for a moment before turning back to the road.

"Nothing, it doesn't matter," I reply, tossing my phone onto the floor.

"Hey, can I ask you about something?" Areon asks, turning down the volume on the radio.

"Yeah." I think about saying that he already did, but I don't want to sound lame.

"Did you..." He trails off, "Never mind."

"No, ask me. What is it?" I say, giving him my full attention.

"I ... did you like it?" He asks.

"Like what?" I ask.

"When I kissed you?" He pauses for a moment, "God, I sound so douchey."

I laugh, "You don't sound douchey. And how do you even know what that means?"

"I heard Andrew saying it when he was on the phone with Gabby one night. Did I use it right?" He laughs.

"Yeah, you did. And yes, I did." My heart pounds in my chest as I think about our secret moment together.

"Nice." He says. I look over at him, eyebrow raised and smirking. "I didn't know what else to say," he laughs, turning the music back up. I grab his hand and intertwine my fingers with his.

"Is this okay?" I ask, he looks down at our hands and smiles.

"Yeah, it's perfect." He tells me.

7

A Hole In The Earth

Darkness swallows the car as Areon pulls off the main highway and onto a dirt road. "Where exactly are we going?" Andrew pops his head into the front seat.

"I've only told you about eight times already." Areon rolls his eyes.

"Yeah, but I wasn't listening those times."

Areon sighs, "We need to get to the entrance to the underworld."

"But couldn't you use your powers to split the earth and drop us in there? Why did we have to drive all the way out here?" Andrew asks, and I can physically feel how annoyed Areon is at this point.

"Because you could die. This way, I open the portal, we walk down some stairs, and we're there. Much easier."

"Could we at least drive with the headlights on?" I ask him.

"No, I don't want to risk anyone seeing us coming."

"Who would be waiting for us all the way out here?" Andrew chimes in.

"The Satanists." Areon and I state in unison.

"Wait, I thought you were kidding about that!" He yells, "Also, can you not say that at the same time next time? Thanks."

"No, they seem to think that this crater is where the angel Satan was thrown to earth from heaven or something like that. They do a lot of weird stuff there." Areon explains. Andrew leans back into the seat, looking as if he's about to be sick.

"Hey, Areon?" I whisper, leaning closer to him.

"Yeah?"

"What's that light up there?" I ask, pointing up the hill. If we had been driving with the headlights on, there would be no way I would have noticed, but about halfway up the horizon in front of us is a small fire. Areon curses under his breath.

"What's wrong?" Andrew groans, covering his eyes.

"Nothing. Looks like we're going to be waiting around for a while."

"Great," Andrew says sarcastically. Areon turns the car and parks behind a bush or a tree, I honestly can't tell which. As he does so, I can vaguely make out two dark figures standing on either side of the fire.

"Do you want to go see what they're doing?" I tease Andrew.

"Funny." He glares at me, and I have to stifle a laugh.

"I'm kind of curious." Areon states, "As long as we don't get seen, I don't think it would be a problem to watch."

"Really? You want to go?" I ask, turning to him in my seat.

"Why's that so surprising?" He asks.

"I don't know. It's a different religion than yours, one that's technically wrong." I say, but I feel stupid as I'm saying it.

"Why would they be wrong?" Areon's raising an eyebrow and staring me dead in the eyes. I almost don't know how to answer him.

"Because you're the proof." I finally say.

"Not really," Areon shakes his head, "They're all right, in their own ways. Every religion can be compared to what's real and have some sort of truth to them."

"That makes sense, I guess. I never really thought about it that way."

"Well, are you ready?" Areon asks.

"We're really going out there?" Andrew groans.

"Come on, scaredy-cat." I laugh.

We walk as quietly as we can towards the direction of the fire, I never noticed how loud Andrew was when he walked before, and if this is him trying to be quiet, I definitely couldn't see how no one heard us coming. The fire is coming from a torch that is aligned with four others all around the top of the crater. Each torch has two cloaked guards standing next to it. Five torches, ten guards. Areon, Andrew, and I hide behind a decent-sized boulder and peek out from the sides to see down into the crater—Well, at least Areon and I do, Andrew hides perfectly center to the boulder and doesn't risk a single look. There's a large pentagram drawn in the middle of the crater and at least ten people in black cloaks standing in a circle around it. Ten deep voices echo over the hill, I can't make out what they're saying at this distance, but whatever it is, they're all saying it at the same time.

"What do you think they're saying?" Andrew whispers, still not daring to look.

"I'm not sure," I answer

"Looks like some sort of sacrifice, I've never actually seen one in person, though," Areon says almost excitedly. I need to remind myself that people used to do this for the Gods hundreds of years ago, and this is probably normal for him.

"Sacrifice," Andrew repeats, I look back at him, and he looks whiter than the moon, his face completely drained of all color. We watch the ceremony for another hour or so before they begin to clear out of the crater.

"Well, it's now or never," Areon says as the cloaked figures disappear on the other side of the crater, the glow of the torches following them as they fade out into the distance.

"You mean we have to go down there after all of that?" Andrew's voice cracks, and it takes everything in me not to laugh. Instead, I grab his shoulder and squeeze it reassuringly. "You'll be fine. You've got us to protect you." I smile and start pulling him down the hill.

While Areon casually strolled down the cliffside not losing his balance once, Andrew and I slid practically the whole way down. If we had tried to sneak down while the cloaked people were still here, they would have caught us in a second.

"Alright, now that we're down here, what are we supposed to be doing?" Andrew says as he wipes the dust from his jeans, I do the same.

"Well, we need to get to the center, but you are not going to like this." Areon stops walking and nods his head towards the center of the crater, but I can smell whatever he's talking about before I even see it. In the center of the crater is a dead animal, with its throat slit.

"Please tell me that's not a pentagram." Andrew groans.

"So, we're going to ignore the nearly headless animal and only focus on the pentagram underneath it?" I ask.

"Yes." Andrew isn't even looking anymore, and he has his t-shirt collar covering the bottom half of his face.

"Alright. So, where are we going next then?" I turn to face Areon, but he's bent over the animal, examining it, "Areon?" I say louder, and he finally stands.

"Sorry, I've got to open the portal to the underworld. One sec." He stands taller and walks a few feet away.

"I thought we couldn't use a portal because it was too 'dangerous' or something," Andrew says, making air quotes with his hands.

Without even turning around or even raising his voice, Areon mo-notonously states, "Different kind of portal," before pressing his hands together and placing them firmly on the ground. He almost looks like he's playing leapfrog until the earth begins to move under him, and he stands back a foot.

Slowly, the earth begins to pull apart from itself, and dust fills the air. Andrew has completely forgotten about the dead animal at this point and is completely entranced by what is happening before us. A small portion of the ground in front of us is now caving in on itself, expanding to about the same length that I am height-wise. It's dark inside, but you can hear the rocks as they bounce down into the hole and around.

Once the ground stops shaking, Areon peers down into the hole and takes a step down into it; it's knee-deep.

"Okay, it's good. We can go down now." He says. Andrew and I both look at each other. "It'll close behind me, so you both have to go first," Areon adds.

"Anything to get me away from the smell of that thing," Andrew motions toward the animal before taking a few steps down into the hole, "How am I supposed to see where I'm going? Its pitch black down here." He adds.

"It's a staircase, once you get far enough, your eyes should add the darkness," Areon tells him. I watch closely as Andrew descends further down the stairs and eventually disappears. "Alright, your turn." Areon turns to me, holding his hand out to help me balance as I step down into the hole.

Andrew was right. It's pitch black and extremely hard to see where I am going, especially when the opening to the staircase closes after Areon and the moonlight is no longer shining down. It's quiet, aside from the sound of our footsteps on the hard-rocky stairs. Areon is a few steps behind me, and Andrew is a few in front of me. The difference between the sounds they make when walking is incredible. Areon is quiet, and I can barely hear him as he makes his way down behind me, but Andrew sounds like a horse running full sprint down the highway. You could probably hear him from a mile away in this silence.

Sixty-three, sixty-four, sixty-five... I have been trying to count every step I take, but I've lost count probably one hundred times because Andrew is so distracting. About halfway down—*I assume because we have been walking for what feels like hours*—he started hopping down the steps instead of walking. Areon was right that our eyes would adjust to the darkness after a while, and Andrew could apparently see better than I could if he is able to hop down and not fall once.

"Man, how much farther?" Andrew whines, and his footsteps stop. I am thankful for the silence before I realize that I can't tell where he is, and he's going to cause both of us to fall.

"Andrew, don't stop! Are you trying to trip me?" I yell and he sighs before I hear his footsteps again.

"I'm so bored, though!" He yells back at me; I am going to have a killer migraine after all of this.

"Stop whining, I told you not to come in the first place," Areon says. At this point, he has been so quiet that I almost forgot that he was even here.

"In all seriousness, though, how much further? It feels like we've been walking for hours." I ask.

"Well, you didn't expect the underworld to be a few feet from the surface, did you? It has to be far in case some dumb human tries to come down here."

"Excuse me, dumb human here. I would have turned around like twenty steps in. Just saying." Andrew sounds even more annoyed than before.

"Sorry, I apologize for the dumb human comment. I'm reiterating what my dad says." Areon says sincerely.

"It's cool," Andrew states, but I could still hear the annoyance in his voice.

We walk in silence for maybe an hour or two. I can't tell how long we have been walking at this point and can barely feel my legs anymore; even Andrew has lost all his energy.

"Hey." Areon says and makes me jump, "We're approaching the bottom. When we get down there—"

"Let me guess, don't look into the light." Andrew interrupts.

"Yeah, how did you—never mind. Do not look at it, you might be able to at first, but the light will get so bright that your eyes won't be able to adjust, and you could go blind." Areon explains.

"Wait, I was right? I was guessing." Andrew laughs, "I guess this is where that saying comes from then."

"What saying?" Areon asks.

"Don't go into the light," Andrew and I say in unison.

"So, people know about this? How? We've never actually had a break in before." Areon starts sputtering out question after question until Andrew has to yell to get his attention back.

"Dude, it's a saying that comes from movies where people die or something. Don't take it so seriously."

"I guess that makes sense; I mean, if you're guessing what happens when you die. Someone had to be right at some point." Areon says, but he sounds like he is trying to convince himself more than he is us.

We start approaching the light a few minutes later. At first, it's dim. Then, gradually, it gets so overwhelming that I could not open my eyes anymore. I let my feet guide me instead. *One step down, another and another.* You'd think that after hours of walking downstairs, you would automatically be able to do it with your eyes closed, but I feel more off-balance than when we first started walking in the dark. I can't help but hold my arms out to the walls of the staircase to try to gain my balance. Instead, I pull down hundred-year-old spider webs and still stumble to find my footing on the stairs. I take a few more steps down before I can't hear Andrew walking in front of me anymore and assume that I've reached the bottom, only to find that I have in-fact *not reached* the bottom of the stairs and can feel my body starting to fall through the air. I hold my arms out, ready to impact with the ground. Instead, I feel an arm wrap around me from behind and pull me back up. Areon is holding me; I'm not sure how he could have seen me fall in this blinding light, let alone manage to catch me out of midair on a steep staircase. *He is a god.* I remind myself; he can probably see perfectly, and I am lying in his arms with my eyes closed, looking like a complete idiot for falling.

He smells like cinnamon, and for a moment, I feel like I am back home in the coffee shop. I miss home. I hadn't realized how much until now, but I enjoyed working in the coffee shop. Even if Jessica never worked hard and kept me there late cleaning up after her. I miss Dad, and school, and Deme. I didn't realize how much I longed for life to go back to normal. Okay, maybe not *normal*, but close to normal, I guess. Going to work, cooking dinner, going to school. Maybe when we get back home, everything could be normal, I guess, but I'm not sure how it would after everything that we have already been through.

"Rose," Areon says, but I'm still lost in thought. Imagining home and the coffee shop. "Rose, you can open your eyes now." He says. I slowly open my eyes, Areon is still holding me, and I'm looking up at him. The light is no longer too bright to bear, and I slowly steady myself on the ground and out of his arms.

The first thing I notice are the glowing crystals that illuminate the underground world like a dimly lit sun. They stick out of the rock ceiling in random patterns that spread to the walls and onto the ground, their different colors reflecting onto the world around us. The second thing I notice is the massive waterfall. I'm not sure what I was expecting, but it certainly was not this. The water is bright blue and is almost brighter than the crystals, causing most of the rock around us to become saturated with the same bright turquoise. The grass beneath my feet is the greenest I have ever seen in my life, and it reminds me of the summers Deme and I spent outside laying in the front yard at night. Nature is blooming from everywhere I look, it is so overwhelming that I can't speak, the words unable to form in my throat.

"It's beautiful," Andrew says in amazement.

"What did you expect?" Areon asks

"Darkness, death, and despair," Andrew replies flatly.

"I guess I can't argue with that too much, considering what we saw on the way in here." Areon turns and walks away from the river, "We should probably set up camp, I can't imagine you guys are up for much more walking." Now that he mentioned it, my legs are shaking, and judging by the exhaustion on Andrew's face, he was pretending not to be in as much pain as he really is. Areon walks away from the water and towards a grassy area surrounded by large rocks that make a sort of cave. He gathers a few larger rocks and begins to place them in a circle before digging the grass in the middle of the rock circle, leaving a small round pit of dirt. Andrew joins us with some small branches, which I am sure are large roots since we're so far underground, and Areon takes them to start a fire. I lie down on the grass and realize how sore my legs are. As I relax them, my legs protest to the lack of movement, and my muscles twitch. I do my best to massage them, and it eases the pain a little, but the twitching doesn't subside. Andrew is digging through his backpack, and he pulls out some chips, granola bars, and his hoodie; he balls it up and uses it as a pillow. He eats a few chips, but exhaustion over-powers him, and he passes out within minutes. Areon doesn't sleep. Instead, he pokes at the fire with a stick. The flames dance in his eyes, and I watch them flicker until I'm overcome with exhaustion myself.

When I wake up, the fire is still burning, but it seems darker out. I look around, and sure enough, the crystals that illuminate the world are dimmed. It must be a representation of the sun. I lift myself up onto my elbows, and while the upper half of my body seems fine, my leg muscles are on fire. It takes too much effort to sit cross-legged, so instead, I sit with my legs stretched out and rub my calf muscles. Andrew is gone, and when I begin to look around for him, Areon responds to my panic with one word, "Bathroom." I relax. I must have been asleep for hours. There is a large pile of sticks next to the fire, and I'm not sure where it came from, but a skinned rabbit cooks on a large flat rock in the fire. I can only tell it's a rabbit because of its ears.

Deme used to have a pet rabbit. I'm not sure where the memory comes from, but I clearly remember her holding a large white rabbit when we were younger. She got it from the state fair. When our mother was still alive and healthy, and Phoenix still lived at home, we used to go every year. We first saw it in the petting zoo, and when one of the volunteers told us that they would have to put the rabbit down because it was old and most children wanted nothing to do with it, Deme knew she had to have it. She begged for days, but we didn't have any pets. Nix always wanted a dog, but Dad didn't believe in having pets, he always said they belong in the wild where they are born, and we didn't argue with him. I guess since we are part wolf, it makes sense. I don't think I could ever own a dog now; it seems unfair. But I guess somehow our mom talked dad into getting Deme the rabbit. They didn't tell her until she got home from school one day. When we got off the bus, and mom walked us home, the cage holding the snow-white rabbit was waiting for us on the porch.

I have never eaten rabbit. It almost tastes like chicken, only earthier. But we haven't eaten in what feels like days, and my stomach is begging me for more. Areon says there will be more food once we get to the castle, but I almost don't believe him. We are here to stop a war, not for a vacation. I can't help but eat more than I need to.

When the sun-crystals begin to brighten, Areon lets the fire die out. We haven't talked much, any of us. The weight of the task at hand must be keeping Andrew's and Areon's minds as pre-occupied as mine. Andrew packs his snacks and hoodie into his backpack again, I can see how tired he still is, but we both know that we need to keep moving. Once the fire is out, Areon leads the way out of the caves and back toward the water. His pace is slower, probably making up for how sore Andrew and I are, but he doesn't say anything. Doesn't even check to see if we are still behind him. He keeps his head forward, and his pace steady.

There is a staircase next to the waterfall that was hidden by moss when we first saw it, but now that we are next to it, it's clear. We make our way up, one by one, to the top of the waterfall.

"Don't touch the water," Areon says sternly as we climb.

"What happens if we do?" I ask. This is the first thing I have said in hours, and my voice is a bit hoarse.

"Darkness, death, and despair," He answers, "Your soul will be ripped from your body, and you will spend eternity in the River Styx. I shiver at his words, and Andrew slides to his left, further away from the splashes of the water bouncing from rock to rock. Beautiful but deadly. When we approach the top of the waterfall, we finally get a good look at the underworld. It is divided into five regions from what I can see, and each section is surrounded by a different river. The castle is in the middle, a bright glowing structure made entirely of the same crystals that illuminate the entirety of the underworld that sits on top of a small mountain. I'm not sure what the other regions contain, though one of them looks like a giant crater, and another looks to be the best of them all.

No one says another word as we travel along the river until we reach a dock. A small boat sits tied to the old wood, rocking gently in the waves. A cloaked figure sits waiting on the boat, his face is hidden by the hood, but I know that this must be the ferryman. Areon steps onto the boat, and a bony hand from the ferryman reaches up to catch three small coins that Areon drops. The bony fingers wrap around the coins greedily, as if one of us is going to attempt to steal them back. Areon holds his hand out to us to help our balance as we step onto the tiny boat. Andrew and I are careful to stay away from the sides of the boat, so we don't touch any of the water. With one final nod, the ferryman begins to row us out into the open water, where it's so foggy we can barely see what is in front of us.

As we reach the shore, the fog begins to clear, and we can finally make out what is on the other side of the river. Cerberus. A giant three-headed dog with serpent-like tails and snakeheads lining its spine. It must be at least somewhat related to the Chimera, although I am not positive. Spirit-like entities are lined up before it, and under it as well as the entrance to the underworld lies right behind the massive beast.

We will not be going this way since none of us are dead. Instead, Areon leads us around the line of souls and through what can only be considered a side entrance, one that is made specifically for the other Gods to use, should they ever need to enter the underworld this way. I am sure that Areon is the only one that uses it though, I'm not sure why I think this though because there is no way to know for sure.

There is another river, and a boat is waiting for us on the other side of the iron gate we use, although no ferryman belongs to this boat; we will have to row it ourselves. We get in, still careful not to touch the water even though Areon hasn't said whether touching this river will give us a similar fate to the River Styx. As we push off from the shore, the current carries us gently down the river, the only time we will need to row is when we need to change direction. Although, it should lead us directly to the castle where we will finally meet Hades.

8

Badlands

We arrive at the middle island in no time at all, where another dock and a marble-like staircase waits for us. Areon ties the boat to a beam on the dock, and we exit the boat.

"Wait," Areon says when we are all finally off the boat and standing on flat ground.

"What's up?" Andrew says, and I realize it's the first time I have heard him speak in hours; his voice is shaky, almost like he is terrified.

"No one can know that Andrew is a regular human," Areon says, his voice barely above a whisper.

"Yeah, we know," I say, my own voice is shaky. I guess I'm more nervous than I thought I was.

"I thought I would remind you." Areon says and turns to the stairs, "These lead to the entrance, I'm not sure where Hades will be, but my mother will be around somewhere. They can't know why we are here either, okay? I mean, they most likely won't ask since you're with me, but don't say anything to them about why you are here." Areon seems nervous too, and I can't help but wonder if it's the first time he has ever done anything like this. I've been standing up to my father for years, but if he were as powerful as the god of death, I probably wouldn't have been so confident saying anything to him.

"We understand, Areon. We won't say anything." I say, and he nods in reply before leading us up to the entrance.

Something stops me halfway up. I'm at the rear, so neither Andrew nor Areon notice for a few moments, but once they do, they come back down to see what is wrong. I shush them when they reach me. I'm straining hard to listen, as my ears are already picking up so many sounds that they probably can't even hear; being half-wolf has some perks. A howl. That's what stopped me, and I hear it again. It calls out, and for some reason, I feel like I know whoever is behind the howl.

"Rose, we need to go," Areon says sternly and reaches out to pull me along, but I brush him off to try to hear it again. It's another wolf; I'm not sure how I know, but if transforming over time gets easier, then my senses are probably getting better over time too. The only problem is that I cannot tell where it's coming from, and Areon is getting increasingly annoyed with how long I'm taking.

"Fine," I say and start following them again. Areon breathes out a sigh of relief, and I can't help but wonder why he didn't want me to listen. He has been different since we got here. The caring side of him is completely gone at this point, and he seems more guarded than I have ever seen him.

We reach the castle entrance in no time, though my muscles are still protesting every step. The crystals that form the castle are much more impressive the closer you are. The rooms inside are carved into the crystals themselves, along with the windows and entryways. They are not as bright the closer you are to them though, I'm not sure if it's because I have gotten used to the amount of light radiating from them. There are also hundreds of plants growing around the castle. Ivy is woven through small cracks in the crystal walls, along with flowers I have never seen before.

"Zagreus, where have you been?" A woman's voice calls out, and the doors before us burst open, revealing one of the most beautiful women I have ever seen. She is fair-skinned with long flowing blonde hair and piercing blue eyes. Her blue gown flows out behind her like the waves of the River Styx, and atop her head is an elegant crown of flowers. I am certain that this is Persephone, Areon's mother. "Oh, we have guests." She says as her eyes lay on Andrew and me.

"I've been out hunting," Areon replies to her, and I'm not sure, but it looks like she smells the air before she seems satisfied with his answer.

"Well, we received the Chimera you sent back. Where on earth did you find it?" She asks.

"A place where humans keep animals for their enjoyment, it's called a zoo. Only Ares oversees it." Areon explains to her.

"Oh?" It's all she says, but I can tell by the look in her eye she is asking for more information. "Well, then. Your father would like to see you. He is up in the throne room. I'll see to it that our *guests* are taken care of." I'm not sure why, but the atmosphere around us feels cold suddenly like there is something going on that I don't quite understand.

Areon disappears up a spiral staircase made of more crystal, and Andrew and I follow Persephone down a series of hallways to a kitchen where she orders some servants to prepare meals for us. We take a seat at a giant polished wooden table, and Persephone pushes the hair out of my face.

"You are a very pretty one, what is your name?" She asks, and I realize that Areon never introduced us.

"I am Rose, and this is Andrew."

"Your full names?" she frowns.

"Oh, pardon me, Rose Knight and Andrew Palmer," I say.

"Knight? You wouldn't happen to have had a family member pass away recently, would you?" She asks, and I find myself amazed that she could even know that since hundreds of people around the world die every minute. Why would she remember my mom out of all of them?

"Yes, actually. It wasn't too recent actually, but my mother died a few years ago." I explain to her.

"Oh dear, well, time works differently down here, I'm sure you are aware." Persephone is smiling, but I can't help the bad feeling that I get from her. Andrew is clearly too mesmerized by her beauty to even speak; he has opened his mouth a few times like he was going to say something but stayed silent instead. When they bring out the food, that's when I lose him completely. There are probably twenty different types of food that sit in front of us. Roast pig, lamb stew, bread that looks the texture of cotton candy, soups of varying flavors, salad that is greener than any lettuce that I've ever seen in my life, the list goes on and on. Andrew is trying to maintain his manners but is struggling to keep himself from shoveling food into his mouth. Persephone doesn't eat with us. Instead, she excuses herself and tells us that she or Zagreus will be back soon.

"This is amazing," Andrew says, between mouthfuls of bread and pork.

"I know, I don't think I have ever seen anything so elegant in my life," I say as I fill my plate for the second time.

"Is that Areon's mom?" He asks.

"Yeah, Persephone," I tell him, he must not pay any attention in English, considering we have been learning about Greek mythology for the last two weeks. Although, at this point, I'm not sure how true anything we have learned so far is. "Should we be calling him Zagreus now?" I ask.

"Maybe, I asked him about it when you were passed out at the hotel, and he said to call him whatever is easiest. But around here, it might be better to call him by his real name." Andrew says, maybe he has been paying attention at least a little bit. We agree that it might be safer to call Areon by his God-given name from now on since Andrew is a human, and we want to cause as little trouble as possible.

Persephone returns as I've finished eating. Andrew is still eating at a steady pace, though.

"I've had some rooms prepared for you and new clothes placed in the closets for you to change into after you've had a chance to clean yourselves off. If you would like to follow me, Rose." She says, and I glance over at Andrew, still eating. "Oh, don't worry, you can finish your meal, young man. A servant will take you to your room when you're ready." She smiles kindly, I hesitantly get up from the table and follow her.

I'm led to a room that looks how I imagine a princess's room might look in a fairytale. A large four-poster bed with silky white fabric that drapes over it, marble floors and a giant stone fireplace, golden rugs with simple designs woven through them. I'm overwhelmed by beauty everywhere I look; I hardly notice when Persephone leaves the room. There is an archway that I can only assume leads to some sort of fantastic bathroom. It does, and my expectations are exceeded when my eyes lay sight on the giant bath in front of me. It's almost the size of a swimming pool, and the faucets look like they used to belong to a pipe organ. Seriously, I could swim laps in this thing if I wanted to. I turn the water on and am overwhelmed by the sounds of rushing water as the pipes fill the bathtub. I'm not sure where the water comes from, but as I take a step into the water, I'm shocked to find the water temperature is perfect. Maybe it's all in my head.

When I'm out of the bath and wrapped in the most luxurious robe I have ever had, I decide to see what clothes are waiting for me in the closet. I was never a dress person, but the dresses hanging in the closet are more than I was expecting. They are all white, or some varying shade of white. Silk and velvet and cotton weave the most beautiful dresses, Deme would die to be able to try one on. I pull out one at random. It is a floor-length dress, which I'm fond of because I don't like to be so exposed. I'm surprised it fits so well when I slip it on, almost as if it is tailored specifically for me. It almost looks like a boho dress made of lace and chiffon. It is form-fitting around my breasts but flows out elegantly at my waist. I look in the mirror in front of me, and I almost look like a bride. I pull the hair on top of my head gently to the back in a barrette, since it's still damp, my natural curls should make an appearance. Normally, I would attempt to straighten my hair, but since there doesn't seem to be any tools here for that, keeping my hair pulled back should help keep it out of my face.

Someone softly knocks on the door. I turn away from myself in the mirror to find Areon–or Zagreus, I guess I should say.

"Hey," I smile, but he seems distracted. "What do you think?" I ask, twirling around, so the skirt of the dress spins around me.

"You look like one of us." He says monotonously, but I can't tell whether it's a good or a bad thing. My smile drops, and I look down at the dress.

"I guess so," I say, defeated. Zagreus crosses the room to me and scoops my face up in his hands, keeping them held on my cheeks.

"You look beautiful."

"Thank you." I blush, and he bends down to kiss my forehead gently. "Where have you been?" I ask.

"Around." He drops his hands, "Trying to get a feel for our situation."

"Oh."

"Yeah, listen." He sighs, "I'm sorry if I've been distant since we've gotten here. I don't really know how to handle this."

"Handle what?" I can tell by his face that he isn't saying something, that he might be hiding something from me.

He sighs, "Everything, I guess. I've never brought guests with me, and my mother is acting strange, I'm not sure if this was a good idea. Bringing you guys here, I mean." He's not looking at me, and I still can't tell if he's being one hundred percent honest with me, but I brush it off and grab his hands.

"I know, I've felt a little different since we got here. But we came here for a reason. We need to stop your father from starting a war." I say in a hushed voice.

"You're right." He squeezes my hands reassuringly before dropping them, "Lay low, okay? I'll try to figure out the best way to approach my parents, and I will let you know where we will go from there. Okay?"

"Yeah, okay." I nod, and he begins to leave before turning back to me in the doorway.

"You really do look like you belong here." He says, and before I have the chance to respond, he disappears into the halls.

I wander around the halls for a while, completely lost, before I run into Persephone again. She smiles at the sight of me.

"You look beautiful, all cleaned up." She says, and I force myself to thank her even though it doesn't feel like a compliment. "I have a surprise for you if you'll follow me." She says. Great. Another surprise. I'm hesitant to follow, but I do even though I get a weird feeling in the pit of my stomach. She leads me around through more hallways and down some stairs. It's no wonder I got lost in the first place. There are so many different hallways and staircases that all look the same. I'm starting to think that she has been leading me around in circles until we reach a door that leads outside.

We step out into a beautiful garden. Roses, lilies, and flowers I have never even seen before line the pathways. As we take a path that leads to another staircase, I look to my left and notice a giant apple tree with the biggest apples I've ever seen hanging from its branches. I'm about to turn away from it when I notice the snake wrapped around the trunk of the tree. So, Adam and Eve were real, after all.

Persephone beckons for me to follow her again since I seem to have become entranced by the snake in the tree. I almost have to force myself away from it, and we begin descending the stairs. These stairs are different, though. They are made of the same crystals that make up the castle and lead to a glowing bridge that I can barely make out in the distance.

We walk for a long time, which makes my calf muscles flare up again. It takes everything I have not to limp because, for some reason, I can't let Persephone see me weak. We walk silently until we reach the bridge, where she tells me that I must continue without her.

"Where am I going, if I may ask?" I say puzzled, the bridge is over one of the rivers, and I'm sure that I'm about to walk into my death.

"You will know when you get there, darling." She smiles innocently. "Cross the bridge and head straight until you reach a gate. Your surprise waits for you there." She doesn't even wait for me to say anything before she turns and walks away, and she never looks back. I'm conflicted. Something tells me that I should listen to her, go straight to the gate, don't look back, but my head tells me not to. Walking any further could result in my death, and I should turn around now. Persephone is out of sight now, I'm not sure how she could have gotten so far away from me in only a matter of minutes, but then again, she is a Goddess. I decide to go with my gut and go to the gate. If I get any bad feelings, then I can turn around and go back.

Once I get to the gate, I lose all feeling. I'm not even sure if I'm breathing and must remind myself to. The giant iron gate in front of me says something in Greek, but it doesn't look harmful. Behind the gate is an empty grass field. What harm could be waiting for me in such an open area? I take a deep breath and unlatch the lock, with one look back towards the castle, I take a step forward and close my eyes.

I open my eyes and look around. *I'm home?* I don't understand. I look behind me to the iron gate and find that the giant iron gate is gone. In its place is a giant ring made of branches and flowers, the center of the ring is filled with a water-like substance that shimmers in the light. Is this a dream? I pinch myself. No. Not a dream. So where am I then? How am I home?

I walk towards my house and realize that—while everything is generally the same—there are things around the house that have never been there. There are flowers growing around the front porch, and there is a tire swing hanging from the tree in the front yard. I walk further up, and as I take a step onto the porch, I hear my name being shouted out. I turn so fast that I get lightheaded and need to grab onto the house's support beam for balance. With spotty vision, I search for the voice because there is no way that it's her. It is impossible. Okay, maybe not entirely impossible considering the things that I've learned the past few weeks, but still.

That's when I see her. Her long, brown hair braided to the side like it always has been. Her olive skin soft against the sunlight. There is not a doubt in my mind that she really is here. I take a step forward, pushing myself off the beam and make my way towards her. Her expression is as shocked as mine is, I'm sure.

"Mom?"

9

Monster

I can't move. Everything in me wants to rush to her, to hug her. I'm afraid, though. Is this some sort of trick? The second I hold her, is she going to disappear? I don't have enough time to think everything through before she pulls me in for a hug, wrapping her arms around me tightly in an embrace that I have longed for, for years. My mother is here. Tears swell in my eyes, but I don't care, because she is here. Here, she is alive. I could have never prepared myself for this.

"Rose, how did you get here. You're not –" She can't finish her sentence, but I'm crying too hard to say anything. Every time I open my mouth to say anything, the most horrible sound comes out of my throat. "Hush, sweetie, it's okay. take a deep breath." She pulls me in for another hug as I take a deep breath, the smell of her perfume is almost enough to make me sob again, but I try to hold it together.

"I missed you." Is all I can manage to say before I see the tears being to form in her eyes.

"I missed you too, pumpkin." She wraps her arm around my shoulders, "Maybe we should go inside." She suggests.

We walk inside, and for the most part, the house completely matches our real home. We sit in the living room, which in our real house is barely touched these days, aside from Deme, when no one else is home.

"So, how did you get here." My mom asks, setting a tray of cookies in front of me, although I get the feeling that I shouldn't eat anything here, so I politely decline.

"I guess it's a long story. I met Areon, only you probably know him by Zagreus." I start, and her eyes go wide.

"So, you remember then?" She asks, and I nod, "How much do you remember?"

"Everything. Okay, most things. A lot is still blurry, but I think that's normal." I tell her and continue to tell her the story of how Andrew and I arrived in the underworld.

When I finish telling her everything, she stops and looks at me with concern.

"So, you aren't here to get your brother then?" She asks.

"What? He's here? How and when? I mean, he ran away a couple of months after—" I stop, I don't want to say it. It doesn't seem right to remind her that she died. She doesn't say anything for a minute. Whether she is trying to find the right words or trying to hide something from me is unclear.

"Your brother came to visit me shortly after I passed." She begins to explain, "You see, your stories are quite similar, the two of you. I'm not sure how or when, this Zagreus had such a change of heart, though."

"Change of heart? What do you mean?"

"Oh, nothing. All I can really tell you is that your brother is here. He has been here for an awfully long time too. Almost as long as I have, but you can get him. You can take him home." I stand up,

I can't believe that after all these years, Phoenix is here. Maybe he wanted to come home, but he couldn't figure out how to get back out. I know that if I had to leave alone, I would probably have a hard time finding my way back to the surface world. I need to find him. I need to get him home.

"Alright." I say, "I'll find him. I will get him home."

"One more thing before you go." My mom stops me as I walk towards the front door. "Don't take out your anger on your father. He went through so much more than you could know. And would you let him know that I love him?" There is so much pain in her eyes that I can't help but tear up again. After all these years wanting to see her again, and I'm all ready to leave after a few moments. Maybe she is right that I've taken out my emotions on my dad but, how couldn't I? He watched her die; he wasn't even home the night she did die. I take a deep breath.

"I'll tell him. Would you like me to stay longer? I'm sorry that I tried to leave so fast." I say, swallowing my pride.

"No, you mustn't stay here too long, or you could risk getting stuck here. I only hope that your brother hasn't fallen victim to such a fate." She says and pulls me in for another hug before ushering me out the door. We say our final goodbyes and hug each other tightly for a few more minutes before I turn away from my home and walk back through the portal.

When I get back to the castle, I decide to find Andrew first. I need to tell him what happened. I find him in the kitchen, still eating, and I'm not sure what time it is, but since the crystals outside seem to be dimming, I can only imagine that it has been hours since I left him here. Has he been eating this whole time? His clothing hasn't changed, and he still has an oily sheen to his hair.

"Andrew?" He doesn't answer me. Instead, he stuffs something pink into his mouth. The plate in front of him is filled with them, small pink pastries that resemble a flower I can't remember the name of. "Andrew!" I say louder and still no response. Since he doesn't seem to hear me, I walk over to the table and pull away the plate of flowers.

"Hey! I was eating those!" He yells loudly. Now that I'm closer to him, he looks sick. His skin seems yellowed.

"Andrew, how long have you been here?" I ask.

"What do you mean? We got here like ten minutes ago." He says groggily.

"No, we didn't." Is all that I can say.

"What? Yes, we did. You only got up a minute ago."

"No, Andrew. We have been here for hours." I explain.

"Really?" His expression goes blank.

"Yes, really. Now come with me, we need to go find my brother." That snaps him out of it.

"Your brother?" he asks, "Phoenix." He says under his breath as he recalls his name.

I fill Andrew in on everything that I have been doing since I left him, only omitting the conversation with Zagreus. He doesn't ask any questions, only listens to my story as we walk back to the garden. When we reach the garden, Andrew seems to be back to normal.

"Okay, so you went to see your mother." He says, "And she told you that Phoenix was here."

"*Is here.*" I correct him.

"But how do you know that? Couldn't he have found his way back out? Why would it have taken six years to climb his way out of the underworld?" He asks.

"Because he got lost or something, I don't know."

"That's unlikely," Andrew says, and he stops walking.

"Why is it unlikely?" I ask. I don't understand why he is being so closeminded.

"Because you already know this place like the back of your hand. I wouldn't know how to get here if I had a map." He explains.

"Yeah, but –"

"No buts. Before you realized you were a wolf, you couldn't even remember which back roads led to your house. You have an excellent sense of direction now. That can only be explained because you are part wolf. And why you heard something that neither Areon—I mean Zagreus—nor I could hear, do I need to elaborate more?" He crosses his arms and raises an eyebrow, begging me to tell him to go on. I can't. Andrew is right, my senses are heightened. My sense of direction, my sense of smell, and my sense of hearing.

My sense of hearing!

I heard something when we got here that neither of them could hear. It was a wolf howling. Why else would a wolf be here? "Phoenix is here." I say, and Andrew rolls his eyes, about to protest, but I stop him, "No, really! When we first got here, I thought I heard a wolf howling for help. That had to be him!" I say, I'm looking around, straining my ears to listen for another howl, but I come up empty.

"Well, if you say so. Let's go find him then?" Andrew says, dropping his arms and walking towards me again.

"Really? You'll come with me?" I ask.

"Well, duh. I've followed you this far, haven't I?" He gestures around us. I smile, pulling him into a hug. "Thank you."

"Should we go find Zagreus first? Maybe he will help us look?" Andrew asks. My heart drops. My mom said something about Zagreus having a change of heart but wouldn't elaborate on what that meant. Did he do something bad? Was all this a trick of some kind? I don't want to believe that. He must be good. Didn't he come here to try to stop a war? Yes, he has to be good. But just in case.

"No, he is supposed to be stopping the war. We can fill him in later."

Andrew and I wander around for a while. I try to listen for another howl or something that will lead us to Phoenix, but it's no use. Instead, I try to smell for something, but I have no idea where to start, and there are so many different smells down underground that I give up on that almost immediately too. It isn't until we start retracing our steps that I finally hear it again. A deep howl from somewhere below the entrance to the castle.

"We should split up," Andrew says.

"What? Why?"

"We don't have to go far, but it will be easier to find a way to him if we both check out different areas." He explains, and I hate to admit it, but he is right. Neither of us really knows where anything is down here, and with both of us checking out different parts of the underworld, we might find Phoenix before Persephone finds us snooping around.

"Fine," I say. "Don't go too far."

We agree that if we get too far apart and can't hear each other, we will meet the other back at the entrance to the castle. I walk back down the steps to where I first heard the howl and begin walking towards where it had come from.

The underworld is getting dark now. Darker than I feel it has been since we got here, but I keep walking. There are plants that I have never even seen growing here. Most of the plants are a type of ivy that tangles itself into the rocks. There are even plants that glow, and they remind me of plankton in the ocean and how they glow at night. More flowers seem to bloom down here too. It is a wonder that all these plants are even alive without sunlight. Although Persephone is known to be the bringer of spring, so I guess it makes sense in a way.

The patterns in the plants are almost perfect, like a seamstress was attempting to weave them into a beautiful blanket. I only see it for a split second, and I'm not sure if Andrew would have been able to catch it if he were the one to see it. The glowing plants have what I can only describe as a surge of energy, sending a ripple down the line of ivy. In a small circle of the vines, a rock glows for less than a second before burning out again, and I take a step back. As I observe the glowing wall, it happens again, and I'm able to clearly see it for what it really is. A doorway.

I signal for Andrew to come to me, and after a few minutes, I hear his heavy footsteps approaching. I show him the plants, and as I suspected, He has no idea what I'm trying to show him until I make him look harder.

"Okay, but how do we open it?" He asks, taking a closer look at the glowing vines.

"I'm not sure, but if I had to guess–" I lean past him and press the center rock when it glows, and sure enough, the wall begins to move. "—Like that," I say proudly while Andrew throws me a look. A portion of the wall slides back and sideways, revealing a dark pathway. Deep growls echo around the cavern, and I can feel a pit in my stomach grow bigger. I get the feeling that Phoenix isn't the only one who could be in this cave.

Candles begin lighting by themselves as Andrew, and I enter the cave, filling the area with a bright light. I am instantly sick to my stomach. There are hundreds of wolves here. Locked in cells and chained to the walls. Bodies line the far side wall; I can't even begin to count how many. I fall to my knees, crying. I can't even remember what I ate last, but it threatens to make a reappearance as I see more and more disturbing images. Some are covered in blood, others in feces, some are sick, and some I can see are so old they look like they might turn to dust any moment. Andrew is saying something, but I can't hear him over the sound of my own cries. I can't believe this. Why are they here, and what are they planning to do to them? Does Zagreus know about them? Hundreds of questions flood my mind as tears flood down my cheeks. I need to help them.

I need to get them out of here. Andrew is shaking me now, desperately trying to get my attention, but I can't focus on him. Everywhere I look, there's something worse than the last. I curl up in a ball on the ground, eyes closed tightly, and put my hands to my ears, so I block out the sounds. I don't want to believe it. There they are. My people trapped and tortured. Is this why Zagreus brought me here? To tie me up and lock me in a cell for the rest of my life? Is the same boy that I grew up with, that kissed me and made me feel loved for the first time, really a monster?

"Rose!" Andrew yells, and I'm forced out of my trance to look up at him. He has also been crying, tear trails shimmer from the candlelight on his cheeks. "I think I found him." He says calmly. I look around, how could he have possibly found Phoenix in this sea of wolves? I'm about to close my eyes again when I see what Andrew is talking about.

One wolf looks younger than the rest, and he is the only wolf that is now trying to rip his chains out of the wall to escape. I stand and shakily make my way to him. He stops pulling at his chains when I get about six feet away and stares intently at me. His eyes are familiar, and I'm not sure if our eyes change when we turn because our dad never mentioned if they did, but there is something familiar about them. They look like our father's when he has been drinking for days, only more feral. I approach him slowly. He has been trapped in his wolf form for years, all the wolves have. This, I'm sure of because, if there was any way they were able to turn human, they would have been able to slip out of their chains easily. The wolf cocks his head to the side and sniffs the air. Good, maybe he will recognize my scent and know that I'm his sister.

"Phoenix?" I call out; the other wolves become silent. "Phoenix, it's me, Rose. Your sister." I explain to him, hoping I can calm him enough to revert. I take a few steps closer to him, holding my hands out in front of me to show that I'm not going to hurt him. "Phoenix, it's me, Rose," I repeat, taking a few more steps forward. He sniffs the air again and, to my surprise, rips his chains from the wall and launches himself at me.

In the amount of time that it takes Phoenix to pull his chains away and land on me, I have already transformed into a wolf. I wasn't expecting the attack, but my body was. I didn't even feel it this time; all the pain that I had felt the first time I changed into a wolf was gone. I guess I was used to it now. Phoenix wasn't expecting me to turn, though, and his aim was too high. He had aimed at my head but had to readjust himself mid-air and is only able to kick my side. I fly to the left, into the bars of a cell filled with other wolves. They don't come after me, though. Instead, they move far away from the bars and huddle close to the wall.

I pick myself up, the wolf is now charging at me again. I dodge to the right, but he grabs me and throws me down to the ground hard. Because he is a male, he can only transform halfway, and because I'm a female, I change into a full wolf. I'm smaller than him, so I should be able to dodge better, but he has the reach of a man and the strength of a wolf. This is going to be a much harder fight than the Chimera, and I don't want to hurt him like I wanted to hurt the other.

I look around for Andrew but can't see him. Hopefully, he retreated out of the dungeon; I can't keep him safe from this if I can't even protect myself. I turn back to Phoenix. He is baring his teeth and standing a few feet away from me on all fours. I bow my head in hopes that he will see that I'm submissive and back down from the fight, but instead, he charges forward again. This time, I'm able to dodge his attack. I run around the outside of the cages and try to put as much distance between us as I can. He moves quickly, though, closing in on me and never leaving his back exposed. I try to replicate his movements of defense. If I can anticipate his attacks, then I should be able to dodge him until he gets too tired to continue. It goes against all my instincts. Nix must be the alpha here, the way the other wolves tuck their tails and bow their heads as he passes them. I am the intruder. The stranger and the threat to the pack, therefore, I need to be eliminated, or I need to take down the alpha. I know I can't though, taking down the alpha means killing him, and I need to bring Nix back home alive.

I'm exhausted. The trek to get to the underworld and the fight are still wearing down on my body. I know that I have already re-broken some ribs from being thrown to the ground, and my left paw hurts where my wrist would be. Probably sprained, but dodging the attacks is much more difficult now. Nix launches again, and I attempt to slide under him, but he catches me mid-air and bites into my spine. I let out a sharp whimper, and he drops me to the ground. I can't move. Am I paralyzed? No, I can still move my legs, but I can feel warm liquid running down the sides of my body and pooling beneath me on the ground. It soaks into the dirt at first, but in a matter of minutes, I'm lying in a mess of my own muddy blood. Nix is standing over me, getting ready for the final blow. The one that will kill me. With one swift movement, I'm in the air again. His claws dig into my skin and puncture tiny holes into my sides. I'm flying and falling through the air as he throws me at a wall. I hit it with so much force that I'm positive I will die here. My vision changes, blurring, and spotting. I can hardly make out the shape of the monster that my brother has become. I look down at my hands. I'm human again. The wolf in me has retreated, knowing that it would be defeated. I close my eyes, not wanting to watch my own blood spill from various points on my body.

"Rose!" I jerk my body up, and a scream falls from my mouth. I open my eyes, and I see three of Areon running towards me. I try to put my hand up to stop him from coming any closer, but he doesn't stop. He is at my side in seconds. He pulls me into him, cradling my broken body into his arms, and he says my name repeatedly. My vision is failing me now, but I strain my eyes to look around for Nix. I'm not sure if it is my imagination or not, but I see him. Not a wolf, but my brother, watching Areon cradle me in his arms. And are those tears on his cheeks? Areon kisses my forehead and squeezes me into him.

The last thing I see is Areon's face before I fade out into blackness.

10

Rescue Me

I wake up on and off for days. I know this because, even though clocks and the sun don't exist in the underworld, my bandages are changed every time I awake, and the people around me are always wearing different clothes. Sometimes, Areon is next to me; other times, it's Andrew. I swear that Phoenix was next to me one night, but he was hidden in so much shadow that I couldn't make out his face clearly.

When I finally wake up for good, I am alone. I'm in the same room that Persephone had taken me to on our arrival, but it feels less inviting in the darkness. Not that I could move if I wanted to. My injuries are so severe that I needed stitches. Instead, I was sewn together by a simple needle, and what looks like a golden thread from a blanket that is so thick I will no doubt have scars from the holes.

The door opens to reveal Andrew and Phoenix.

"She's awake!" Andrew exclaims as he runs over to the side of my bed. Phoenix hangs back by the door, hesitant to step any further. "How are you feeling?" Andrew asks.

"Broken." Is all I can say, my throat is sore.

"That's to be expected," Andrew says before he waves for Phoenix to come join us. Now that he is closer, I can see the damage that he has endured. He is bruised and so skinny that I can't help but feel like his bones are going to pop out of his skin. The clothes he wears are much too baggy, although I almost think that might be the point of them. To hide how malnourished he is. He has cleaned since that night in the cave. His long, dirty blonde hair is curling in different directions, the same way mine does after I wash it.

"Rose, I—" Phoenix chokes, his voice is stronger than I remember, deeper. "—I'm sorry." He continues, "I didn't know it was you until..." he stops there. I can see the hurt on his face, and I know that he really is sorry. I nod, not wanting to use my voice, which they seem to understand.

"We need to talk to you about something," Andrew says, shooting a look I don't understand at Phoenix, "You up to listen?" He asks, and I nod again, unsure what they could possibly want to talk to me about. "Phoenix has been here for the last five years." Andrew starts, and I raise an eyebrow. We already know this; if we hadn't, we wouldn't even have gone looking for him.

"I don't remember much from before." Phoenix continues, "I remember mom dying, and I remember dad fighting with me because I wanted to drop out of school."

"What?" I ask, "I didn't know that."

"Yeah, I was already failing because of the amount of time we spent in and out of the hospital. First, because you lost your memory and then because mom got sick. I fell behind in my schoolwork, and before I knew it, I was failing everything. Dad wouldn't let me, and we fought. I pushed him, and because he was drunk, he told me to get out, and I did." Phoenix sighs, "I was going to come home, but I went to that stupid fort that you built with your friends. That's when I met Zagreus." He looks me in the eyes and decides whether to keep going. "The next thing I know, the earth opens up, and he drags me down here against my will." My heart drops to my stomach, and I think I might faint. Why would he do that? Why would he take my brother away?

"Why?" I ask.

"I don't know, but he did the same thing to the other wolves. Maybe to build an army or something. It doesn't matter now. Now that you're here, you guys can help me get them out. Rose, we need to save them." Phoenix explains, and my mind starts racing. An army? The battle between Gods. Hades. The end of the world. It all begins to click into place, piece by piece. Hades sent Zagreus to gather an army, an army of wolves, to fight the other Gods; to end the world. Zagreus is the reason my brother left. The reason I had to give up on everything to take care of my sister. To make sure that we didn't end up in foster care. It's all his fault. I'm crying because I feel so betrayed. How could he do this? Come to me and tell me about the war, about wanting to stop it, when he is the reason that it would take place. I never want to see him again.

We go over a strategy. We need to find a way to get all of the wolves out of here safely and without anyone noticing. We all agree that the only way out is to go the way that Andrew and I came in since none of us can conjure up a portal to the real world. Even if we could, we still don't know if Andrew would survive since he is only human. Cerberus won't let anyone leave, so we will need to take the back way that Zagreus showed us. But will the wolves even come with us? Phoenix says that there are wolves that have been here their entire lives and some that are eighty years old. For some of them, the underworld is all they know. Phoenix should be the one to get them; he is their alpha after all. They will have to listen to him. We stop briefly as a servant comes in to check my bandages, only to find that they have, for the most part, completely healed. It will be a trip to escape since I still have a few broken ribs. Fighting is out of the question for me, though, so I will need to stay close to the pack in case we get attacked.

We get called to dinner, and since I want to know if I can manage walking, I join them in the dining room. It's strange that I haven't seen Persephone or Zagreus since I woke up, but I'm glad. I'm not sure what I would do or say if I saw either of them anyway. I can walk fine; only occasionally, I get winded and need to slow down. But by tomorrow, I should be better and faster. Eating is easier than I thought it would be since my throat is so sore, I can keep everything down. We make sure to avoid the little pink flower pastries that Andrew had been eating. We aren't sure what exactly they are, but the way Andrew described them, he said it was like being drugged. After dinner, we head our different ways to go to bed. We need our rest for tomorrow, especially me. Tomorrow we save the wolves and go home.

I'm restless and spend most of the night tossing and turning. Even when I do sleep, my head is full of unanswered questions that lead to nightmares. Areon and I standing on the cliff and him kissing me before pushing me off, werewolves clawing their way from under the ground and killing innocent people, and fires as far as the eye can see are a few dreams that haunt me into staying awake. Morning can't come soon enough.

When the morning does finally come, I have only gotten three hours of sleep. I climb out of bed and into the bath before digging through the closet to find my old clothes. Andrew and Phoenix creep silently through the halls and make their way to my room soon after. We go over the plan one last time.

I will open the doorway to the cavern of wolves, but Phoenix will go in first. He will be the one to tell them we are leaving and begin to unchain them. Andrew will stay by the door to keep watch, and I will stay close behind Phoenix to show them that I can be trusted. Once everyone is unchained, we will lead them to the river that goes around Cerberus. Hopefully, most of them, if not all, will be able to revert to their human form so we can fit more of them onto the boat at a time. Since there is only one boat, we will need to make multiple trips. The ferryman will have returned to the other side of the Styx, but Andrew noticed multiple boats on our side of the shore, so we should be able to row ourselves back to the water-fall, and then it is the stairs and freedom.

When we get to the cavern, the door is already open. We cautiously make our way inside, only to find Zagreus waiting for us. To my surprise, though, he is letting the wolves out of their cages.

"What are you doing to them?" Phoenix calls out as Zagreus drops the chains from another cell door.

"I am helping you," Zagreus says.

"Helping us? You are the reason they are all here in the first place. Why would you want to help?" Phoenix asks. He looks like he is going to turn any second.

"Is that what you think?" Zagreus asks and turns to us, "That I want to capture you and lock you away for the rest of your lives? Is that what you think, Rose?" I look away, I haven't had much time to think it over, but I know that he is the reason for most of my heartache. "If I hadn't brought your brother here, if I hadn't taken him to your mother, you would have had no reason to find them, the others would have been killed, the second you challenged Hades to end the war," Zagreus explains. "Please, let me help you."

I want to believe him; everything in me is telling me to trust him, but I can't. He kidnapped innocent people, my brother, helped destroy my life. How can I trust someone that I hardly know? Because I like him? Because I *love* him? I don't know. He has been hiding things from me since the moment I met him. I look at Andrew and can see that he is having the same dilemma as I am. Phoenix, on the other hand, wants nothing to do with him. My heart says one thing while my head is saying another.

"I'll prove it to you." Zagreus finally says. He walks away from the cages and the other wolves, into the center of the cave. He claps his hands and places them to the ground the same way that he did when we first entered the underworld. The ground shakes, and the dirt begins to split apart. Only instead of a staircase, there is a glowing blue portal. The same kind of portal that I saw when I visited my mother. "There, this portal will take each person back to where they were taken from." He says, standing and walking over to us.

"How do we know it won't kill them?" Phoenix spits.

"Why would I do that? How could I be so evil in your eyes that I would kill these people?" Zagreus fires back. "I don't want anyone to get hurt! Why else would I bring Andrew and Rose here, to kill them? You don't even know what I had to go through to get them to let you out of this cave, Phoenix. Why would I want to kill the only people who have ever treated me as something other than a God?" He has a point. Before I knew that Areon was really Zagreus, all I wanted was to be his friend, maybe even more at some point. I didn't even consider the risk he had to take to get his parents to let Phoenix out.

"We should trust him," Andrew speaks up.

"Really? You're going to take his side?" Phoenix turns on him.

"No, Phoenix, but he has a point," I say, the betrayal in Phoenix's eyes is almost too much to bear. "It will take them all home faster than we were planning to," I explain, Zagreus walks over to me, reaching out for my hand. "Don't touch me." I pull away, "I may be trusting you now, but that doesn't mean I'm not angry with you." I say to him.

"I'm sorry. I know that I have a lot to make up for, but please, trust me, Phoenix. I will get them home safely." Zagreus says, hurt clearly in his eyes. I can see Phoenix considering every option as his eyes comb over the entire room.

"Fine," Phoenix says, and he turns to the wolves. He nods at them and begins taking their chains off.

"The chains were enchanted to keep the wolves from reverting to humans," Zagreus explains, "They should revert before entering the portal. I'm not sure where exactly each one is going, but the odds are that some of them will return in broad daylight. We still need to protect the secret that werewolves exist."

"Agreed," Phoenix says monotonously before turning himself back to a wolf.

Now that we are on the same side and he isn't attacking me, I can really see what kind of wolf Phoenix is. He is taller and more muscular, but that's about the only difference between his wolf form and his human. In fact, this is the same as the rest of the wolves. As they become their human selves, each of them stays roughly the same skin color they were as a wolf, and their hair color remains the same as well.

"Rose, how come you look so different from them?" Andrew whispers. I think back to what my dad taught me. Male wolves have less self-control, so they only become hybrids. Stuck somewhere between man and wolf. Women can completely turn. I tell this to Andrew, who listens politely.

"But most of them have the same fur color as their hair color, and you don't," he states.

"I don't?" I think back to when I first turned, how thick black patches of hair began to grow all over my body, I'm not sure why I didn't think about it then, I think maybe because it was so dark and after that, I didn't pay enough attention to it. "What color am I?" I ask.

"Black. Almost like a shadow." Andrew says.

"I don't know." I can't remember my dad saying anything about different colored wolves.

When all the wolves have reverted, I feel even sicker than the first time I saw them. Most of them are old men. Originally, I'd thought Phoenix was the youngest of them all; now, I see there are children. I can't see any women, though.

"You kidnapped children?" I say under my breath. I don't want Zagreus to explain. I'm sick to my stomach already, and there is no way he could justify kidnapping children.

"I know it's wrong, and I didn't want to do it. There isn't any excuse, but I didn't have any choice." Zagreus says.

"There is always a choice," I state.

Now in their human states, the people begin to cower together. Many of them were taken while in their wolf form because they have no clue how they got here or where they even are. Phoenix begins to order them into the portal, but they don't obey.

"Why won't they go?" Andrew asks.

"For many of them, this is the only life they've known. They are afraid to leave." Phoenix says, but he doesn't need to tell me. I can see it in their faces.

"I know you are all afraid and confused. But the best thing for you is to go home." I say to them.

"What about those of us who don't have homes to return to?" An elderly man asks, he is one of the oldest in the crowd. Seventy, maybe eighty years old. My heart aches for him.

"I know that this is scary, I know that most of you probably won't have homes to return to, but if you stay here, the Gods will use you as a weapon or kill you. Is that what you want? To be a puppet to the Gods? To never live your lives the way you want?" I ask them. They discuss what I have said among themselves until a child, no older than twelve, steps forward.

"Will I get to see my mommy?" He asks, and tears form in my eyes as I kneel forward to hug him.

"Of course you will. All you need to do is step down into that pretty pool of water, okay? When you come back out, your mom will be looking for you." I say to him. In a way, he reminds me of Deme. His hazel eyes reflect the same loss that hers did when we lost our mother. "Come on, I'll hold your hand, okay?" I hold out my hand for him, and he takes it. We walk to the portal hand in hand before he turns to me one last time.

"Thank you." He says, and I hug him tightly, before helping him step down into the portal. I only let go when the top of his head has disappeared inside it. When I look back up, everyone is staring at me, and there isn't a dry eye in the cave; even Zagreus has tears in his eyes. The people decide they can trust me after that. I help them, one by one, into the portal, holding each of their hands as they step through. Even the eighty-year-old man steps through the portal, thanking me as he does.

As the last person enters the portal, I turn to Phoenix. "Are you ready to go home?" I ask. Before he has the chance to answer, the portal closes. We turn to Zagreus, but he looks as shocked as we all do.

"What's going on?" Andrew asks.

"We need to get out of here," Zagreus says.

"What, why? What is happening?" I ask, making my way over to him.

"The only other people who can close these portals, are my parents. They know what we've done. We need to leave. Now!" Zagreus runs to the doorway and stands between it like you would hold an elevator door to open for someone, and the rest of us rush out. When he pulls away from the doorway, it slams shut, and the glowing vines begin to die out.

"Avoid the paths and get to the boat as fast as you can," Zagreus orders us, and we obey. For Phoenix and me, jumping the rocks and plants is simple, but Andrew is having trouble. I wait for him and then force him to get on my back, he doesn't have time to fight me on this because it's not a second later we hear the howls.

"Hellhounds!" Zagreus calls out, "Get Andrew out of here!" I obey, grabbing Andrew and pulling him through the bushes instead of over them and around the rocks. It is slower than if he were to get on my back, but we are out of time.

We emerge onto the dock a few minutes behind Phoenix and Zagreus, who are already waiting on the boat for us. I don't dare to look back, and I refuse to let Andrew go behind me. The pounding of the hellhounds' paws on the wooden dock behind us is enough to push us forward. I throw Andrew onto the boat, not caring if I get splashed by the water and jump in after him. Phoenix and Zagreus push the boat away from the dock but aren't fast enough. An enormous black dog lunges for Phoenix, only to get pushed away by Zagreus and thrown into the water. Andrew and I shield ourselves from the backsplash, but through the cracks in my fingers, I can see the effects of the water on the mutt. It is almost like the dog was dropped in acid. Flesh drips from the dog as it shoots itself forward out of the water. As the dog swims for the shore, its body begins melting into the water until there is nothing left. Zagreus begins to paddle away, while the other hellhounds are sizing up the jump it would take to reach the boat, but quickly give up.

We go farther than we need to, to avoid Cerberus. Although, Zagreus is positive that they wouldn't send him after us. Hades couldn't afford to lose his guard dog, and Cerberus is a very anxious animal anyway. Whatever that means. We travel an extra mile down river and must jump over a wall to get to the second dock. No one is waiting for us, which seems strange, but I welcome the relaxation that comes with not having to run.

Everyone remains quiet as we travel across the main of the Styx to the waterfall. We have been lucky not to get hurt by anything this far, and I'm sure that no one wants to jinx it; I know I don't.

"I don't get why you can't open another portal," Phoenix grumbles at Zagreus. He is clearly not happy that we have decided to trust him, even though Zagreus saved his life from the hellhounds.

"Because we don't know if Andrew could survive it. I've never used a portal on a human before." Zagreus explains, returning the attitude. We ride the rest of the way in silence.

When we reach the shore and step off the boat, I hear them again. The hellhounds. Zagreus and I make eye contact before taking off towards the stairs. I grab Andrew's wrist and begin pulling him, and he doesn't resist. Since the terrain here is much smoother, it's easier for him to keep pace with me. We run down the stairs to the side of the waterfall and race to the exit as fast as we can.

Phoenix gets to the staircase first and begins to ascend to the surface world, Zagreus follows behind him but waits on the first step for Andrew and me. I grab Andrew's wrist again when he begins to slow down. His breath is rapid, and I can feel his heartbeat in my hands as we make way for the stairs. *A few more feet.* I grab Zagreus' hand, and he pulls me up onto the first step, only for me to be dragged backwards onto the hard ground. I look behind me, expecting to see Andrew being dragged away by a hellhound. Instead, it seems like a glass barrier has been placed between us. Andrew pounds on the barrier, trying to get in, but it is no use.

"Andrew!" I pound on the glass barrier, desperately trying to get to him. I can't leave him here. I won't leave him here. Tears pour down my face as I punch the glass, I'm bleeding, but that doesn't stop me. Someone pulls on my shoulders, trying to get me away from the barrier. "Areon, help me!" I say through my sobs, "We can't leave him!" Andrew is crying too. He has given up on trying to break the barrier and rests his hands on it; I place mine on his as if somehow, we are touching and sob into the barrier.

"You didn't think that I would let you waltz out of here with all of my warriors and not take anything in return, did you?" A woman's voice calls out. I look up to find Persephone standing behind Andrew. Andrew doesn't look at her, though. Instead, his eyes stay focused on mine. "No. I think I'll keep this one." Persephone smirks, the look on her face makes me want to tear her throat out. Zagreus is trying to pull me back again, but I don't budge. When he lets go, I can hear him open a portal behind me, but I don't turn. I look at Andrew again and try to take in everything I can about him. His dark skin, the naturally curly hair on top of his head, splayed out in different directions, and lastly, his eyes. His golden eyes. They have the tiniest brown flecks in them, like little freckles; I never noticed them before. A tear rolls out from them and down his cheeks as he mouths the word *go*.

That's when I lose it.

Tears pour out of my eyes, and I can hardly see anything anymore. "I'll come back for you!" I cry out. Persephone is laughing, but I don't care. "I will find a way to bring you back." Zagreus is pulling on me again, "I promise, I will be back for you!" both Zagreus and Phoenix are pulling me back now, "I promise!"

The only thing I can focus on as I'm pulled backwards through the portal is the small glimmer of hope in Andrew's golden freckled eyes.

11

Blinding Lights

I am so blinded by the sun; I want to rip my eyes out. I fall onto the ground and shield my eyes as even more tears pour from them.

"We left him there," I say to no one.

"We didn't have a choice, Rose," Zagreus says to me, his hand rests on my back, but I roll away from him.

"There is always a choice." I sob into my hands.

"I hate to admit it, but he's right, Rose," Phoenix says from somewhere farther away. I peek out from my hands, and as my eyes adjust to the light, I realize that we are back by Zagreus's jeep.

"Why didn't you take us home?" I ask Zagreus as calmly as I can manage.

"I didn't want to risk them tracking us down." He says, shrugging his shoulders.

"They are Gods, doesn't that make them more than capable of tracking us down?" I ask, but Zagreus ignores me and walks to the jeep.

"Let's go." He orders. Phoenix offers me a hand up, but I ignore him.

"I'm not going. Leave me here." I tell him.

"Don't be ridiculous, Rose." Phoenix rolls his eyes at me.

"Don't be ridiculous? Coming from the guy who, ten minutes ago, wanted nothing to do with Zagreus. You don't have room to talk." I spit.

"Since when do you call me Zagreus?"

"Since you ruined my life." I glare at him, but he doesn't turn away. We stare at each other, neither one of us backing down until Phoenix stands between us.

"This is childish," He says to me, "Get in the car, we are leaving."

"I'd rather die," I say, turning my anger to him. He hasn't been back in my life for more than a few hours, yet he already believes that he can control me. That I'll submit myself and let him become my alpha. No, thank you. To think that either of them can tell me what to do is laughable. I stand up and brush the dirt from my pants. "Neither of you owns me. I can do what I want. And what I want is to save my friend from the underworld. If I have to dig my way back down there, I will!" I turn around to walk away but get cut short by a sharp pain to the back of my head.

"You didn't have to hit her!" Zagreus yells as my ears begin to ring. I can only make out their figures as I pass out into the blackness.

My dreams are haunted by hellhounds killing Andrew repeatedly.

I wake up in the back seat of Zagreus' jeep. I try to stretch out my legs, but there is hardly enough room for two people to sit back here, let alone one person to sleep comfortably. It is dark outside now and impossible to tell where we are. Zagreus is driving, and Phoenix sits in the passenger seat next to him. Neither is talking, and no music is playing. I stare at the two of them. It is a sight that I never thought I would see, like two worlds meeting.

"Where are we?" I ask groggily.

"Oh, she's awake." Phoenix says, "I thought you would be out until we got home."

"Where are we?" I repeat.

"A few miles out of Paradise," Zagreus says. I sit up to look out of the windows, my head still hurts, but I ignore the pain to try to look around. Sure, enough, I see a sign: **Paradise 15 miles**.

"I slept the whole way back?" I ask rubbing the back of my head. There is a bump the size of a golf ball.

"Not the whole way; you woke up a few times screaming." Zagreus calmly states.

"Oh," I look down at my hands, "I don't remember."

"Of course you don't. Your darling brother here hit you over the head with a rock." Zagreus glares at Phoenix for a moment before turning back to the road.

"Hey, we both were thinking about it. There was no other way she would have come with us!" Phoenix defends himself.

"We both were *not* thinking about it. We could have talked to her." Zagreus says to him. They have clearly fought about this while I was unconscious, judging by how coldly they are treating each other. I was so devastated, I'm not sure if talking to me would have worked though. The thought of Andrew sitting in the underworld makes me tear up again, so I push the thought out of my mind.

"What are we going to do when we get home?" I ask, "How are we supposed to–" I stop myself; I can't bear to think about covering up what happened to Andrew. I feel like a murderer. I shouldn't have let Andrew come with us in the first place. His death is on my hands.

"We will discuss it when we get back to town. We have another issue we need to figure out first." Zagreus tells me.

"What is that?" I ask. I have no idea what he could mean until he gestures to Phoenix.

"What are you going to tell people about Phoenix? Where has he been the last five years?" He says, and I have to think hard. Dad never reported him as a missing person. When people asked me where he went, I usually avoided the question, the only person I ever talked to about him was Andrew.

"Dad will know what to do," I say.

"What, that drunk?" Phoenix snorts, "Good luck getting him to care."

"What are you talking about, Phoenix? Of course he cares!" I tell him. "He wouldn't even let us go into your room in case you came home." Phoenix ignores me and looks out the window. I look at the clock on the dashboard—midnight. Hopefully, dad will still be awake when we get there.

I can see why he doesn't want to trust him. Phoenix is right. Dad was never there for us. He was always too drunk to even think about his kids, let alone the one who ran away. But I have to have some faith in him. I left Deme alone with him, and I can only hope that he has taken enough responsibility to at least buy food for her. I can't wait to see Deme. The longest we have ever been apart was during school, and even then, we saw each other in the hallways. It's the thought of seeing her that is helping me stay sane. I can't imagine how she is going to react to seeing Phoenix. Will she forgive him for leaving or be as angry with him as I was? And how will dad react? Only time will tell.

We pass the stoplight that serves as the entrance to Paradise. A casino, then some gas-stations and the movie theater. I could draw a nearly perfect map of Paradise if you asked, but Phoenix looks like he is lost. His head darts around in different directions as he looks around town. I try to think back about what buildings are new, that he wouldn't recognize, but Paradise has remained the same over the years. I can tell he doesn't remember any of it, though. I recognize the look on his face as the same look I had on mine for years. Losing your memory of the things you love takes a toll on your mind. There were many days when I couldn't remember where I lived, who my parents were, where I went to school. I hated myself for not remembering. Especially when our mom died. Some days, I thought about running away myself, and I would have if it weren't for Deme.

Phoenix says nothing as we pass through town. No one is out on the streets, but you can hear the shouts of people from the local bars that we pass. Nightlife in Paradise doesn't really exist. There are no nightclubs, only bars and a lot of them. The Bison bar and grill seems to be the most popular, but there are bars in most restaurants too that are equally as popular. Although only a few restaurants remain open at this hour. Occasionally, Phoenix will look at something like he remembers it. It is short-lived, though, as we drive through town.

It takes fifteen minutes to get from one end of town to get to our house, and as we pull into the long dark driveway, I sigh in relief when I see the kitchen light on. Someone is awake, and Dad's truck is in the driveway. There is a fifty-fifty chance that he is the one awake. We park behind Dad's truck and sit for a minute. Phoenix has gone from looking like a lost puppy to a petrified ghost. He sits perfectly still, staring at the house, not making any movements towards getting out of the vehicle. Zagreus and I look at each other before he gets out and pulls his seat forward so I can too. I make my way over to the passenger side when I notice Phoenix is shaking his head. I open the door, and he immediately tries to pull it shut.

"I can't go in there." He says.

"What do you mean? We came all this way, you have to." I tell him.

"No, I can't."

"Why? Because you're scared? If you can travel to the under-world, become the alpha of a pack of wolves, and make it out alive, you can go see your family." I argue with him.

"He is going to kick me out again." He says, and I roll my eyes.

"No, he won't," I say. But he doesn't have much longer to figure out what he is going to do, because I can see movement by the door out of the corner of my eye. "I'll be here the whole time," I say, holding out my hand. The front door opens, and I can hear footsteps. Phoenix grabs my hand reluctantly and gets out of the car. I turn to see our father standing on the porch. He has a gun in his hands.

"It's okay, dad. It's us." I call out to him. He drops the gun and starts over to us. Judging by the fact that he isn't falling over, he isn't drunk. Phoenix and I make it about ten feet away from him when dad stops in his tracks. He observes us, Phoenix and me, hand in hand, and I'm not sure, but I think I see tears swelling in his eyes.

"Boy." He says, holding his arms out. Phoenix drops my hand and embraces our father. Dad says something to him, but I can't make it out. A light turns on in my bedroom window, and I can see Deme, groggily peeking out of the blinds. I wave at her before she quickly disappears. Moments later, she comes running out of the door and into my arms.

"I've missed you so much!" She says.

"I missed you too," I hug her tightly, "But I think someone else might want to see you." She turns to where dad and Phoenix are, and gasps before going over to them and joining in on their hug. Forgiveness, I should have known. Deme has always been the more kind of the two of us. She isn't the grudge-holding type.

Zagreus comes over to me as I'm watching my family reunite.

"We have something else we need to figure out." He says, and I nod.

"I'll be back. There is one more thing I need to do." I call out to my family.

"Do you want me to come with you?" Phoenix asks.

"No," I shake my head, "You stay here and catch up, I won't be long," I tell him. Zagreus and I get back into the jeep, and as we pull out, I watch them go into the house and disappear behind the front door.

Rain pours from the dark sky as Zagreus, and I make our way to his house.

"Are you okay?" He asks.

"I'm as good as I can be," I tell him. I reunited my family at the cost of my best friend. I hate myself. But Zagreus doesn't need to know that.

"I'm sorry." He says. I look at him sideways, unsure of what he could be apologizing for at this point.

"For what?" I ask.

"For everything. I should have told you the truth from the beginning. I don't know why I didn't. I guess I didn't want you to see me as a monster." He sighs, "But I guess you saw me that way anyway."

"I don't see you as a monster," I say, surprising myself.

"You don't need to lie to make me feel better." He says. We pull into his driveway a minute later; Andrew's truck is still there waiting for us. "You drive my car, and I'll lead the way in Andrew's truck." He says, pulling Andrew's car keys out of the backpack Andrew had left behind.

"I can't drive," I tell him.

"You don't need a license; no one is going to catch us." He says.

"No, I don't know how to drive." I explain, "I never learned." Zagreus sighs.

"I guess we'll both go in Andrew's truck then and walk back." He says.

"What are we going to do with the truck?" I ask.

"Drive it into the river." He tells me.

I hate this plan. Making Andrew's death look like a suicide. He isn't even dead, only trapped in the underworld. I guess that's the same thing. We drive in silence to a wide creek that is overflowing. It must have been raining for days, for the river to be running this fast. We get out of the truck, and Zagreus puts Andrew's backpack in the front seat. I place his cell phone in the center console, where he always kept it. I back away from the truck as Zagreus follows through with the rest of the plan. We will leave the car running and put it into drive; since the truck is on a hill, it should drive itself into the river bed, where the rushing currents of water will push it and make it look like the body was washed away.

I watch as Zagreus places the truck into drive, he presses the gas to get it going and gets out. We watch the truck rush down the hill together, the mud flies from under the tires. When the truck hits the water, it looks like an explosion. Water flies from every direction at least ten feet high. When it settles, the truck chokes out and dies.

"Goodbye, old red," I say to the truck before we start the walk back to Zagreus jeep.

The walk would be short on a clear day, but because of the mud and rain, it is going to take us half an hour, at least. We don't say anything to each other. Instead, I listen to the sounds of the rain hitting the leaves in the trees. I focus on the smell of the wet foliage, and I can't believe we did that. Andrew's mother and father are out of town, and I'm not sure when his mom will be back either. I think back to the day she left for California. How tightly she had held me. Mrs. Palmer treated me like her own, and I got her son taken and destroyed his truck. I will never be able to look her in the eyes again.

"I can make you forget if you want," Zagreus says, interrupting my thoughts.

"What?"

"I can make you forget about him. Andrew. Not everything, but I can make you forget leaving him behind." He offers.

"Why would I want that?" I stop walking, "Why would I want to forget him?"

"I don't know. To make it easier. If the cops question you or something–" he starts, but I cut him off.

"Oh, so you think that I will blow your cover with the cops. That I will tell the whole world that the Gods exist, and they kidnapped my best friend. So, you drove his truck into a river to hide that there is no body. You are unbelievable! I can't believe you would even offer that." I yell, the rain gets into my eyes, fogging my vision.

"Rose, that's not what I–" He reaches out for me, but I pull away.

"No, I should've expected this. You thought you could lie to me about my brother and the end of the world too, why wouldn't you want to erase my memory?" I laugh even though I'm crying now. "You don't think I can get him back, do you? That's why you brought me back here, that's why you offered."

"Rose."

"You're wrong. I will bring him back. I will bring him home, like my brother. I don't know how, but I'll do it! Go mess with everyone else's memories. I don't want to see you anymore." I don't wait for his response, and instead I turn into a wolf and take off.

I want to run as far away and as fast as I possibly can from here.

12

Burn It Down

I stare at the ceiling in my bedroom. I have been for days, maybe even weeks; honestly I'm not even aware of what day it is anymore. Deme brings me food, and Dad tries to have conversations with me through the door. Phoenix doesn't come at all, which doesn't surprise me; he has three years' worth of homework and friends to catch up with. I watch tv occasionally; a week ago, the news started reporting that hundreds of missing people were turning up around the world. The wolves must have finally returned home and settled in, why they would be interested in doing interviews for the media is beyond me.

That was when we told Deme the truth about everything. Dad explained that we were wolves, and Phoenix told her about what happened after he ran away, I told her the rest. She didn't ask many questions; she accepted that we told the truth hole-heartedly. I only omitted the details about Zagreus and me. No one needed to know about the kisses or the hand holding, and they didn't need to know about the fight we got into after we destroyed Andrew's car.

We hid Phoenix for a while. It seemed rude to bring up that our missing brother had come home when the Palmers were busy trying to find their son. Eventually, we needed to tell people that Phoenix had come home, though. It only made Andrew's mother more hopeful. I haven't seen them, Andrew's parents. Dad sees them in passing, though, and even volunteered to be a part of the search party for Andrew's body. They asked me to help look, but I couldn't bring myself to do it. Not when I knew there was nobody out there, that he was somewhere in the underworld.

After a couple of weeks of searching, the police refused to help any more. They had wasted hundreds and thousands of dollars on sweeping every river and lake that branched off from where they found the truck. They assumed his body was lost to the river. It was Andrew's dad that had decided to call off the search parties. If it had been up to his mom, they never would've stopped looking.

There is a knock on the door, but I don't answer it. I stay staring at the ceiling in my room. Trying to figure out a way to bring Andrew home like I have been. Deme comes in and sits on the edge of my bed. She ignores looking at me for a few minutes and seems to be judging on whether she should say what she came in here for.

"Are you going to shower?" she asks.

"For what?" I ask, my voice is raw. I don't think I have talked in days.

She hesitates, playing with the edge of my blankets. "Andrew's funeral is today." She says.

The funeral.

This was Andrew's dad's idea, as well. Although, without a body, they are burying an empty casket. They are doing it to make peace with themselves; that's what dad had said when he told me about it. I must go. There would be no argument about that. I needed to go to support his parents, to help them grieve. I am one of Andrew's closest friends or *was*. I'm still not sure how to talk about him. Past tense or present tense, that is. Technically, he is still alive, he is trapped in the underworld, working as a slave or whatever they are making him do down there.

"Yeah, I'll shower in a minute," I tell Deme, and she leaves the room. My muscles are stiff. Since I have been in bed for almost a week now, the only exercise I get is when I have nightmares and wake up thrashing around my bed, which seems to be every night now.

The shower is cold and successful at pulling me out of my tired trance. My hair is tangled since I haven't been brushing it, and I use my fingers to rip apart the wet knots. I watch a few clumps circle the drain before disappearing all together.

I find a black dress waiting for me on my bed when I get out of the shower. I recognize it as one of Deme's. It is almost the same as the dress I found in my closet in the underworld. Fitted around the breast and flows down to the floor, only this dress is black. Even the jewels that line the dress are black. Deme comes in to do my hair. As she does, I look at myself in the mirror. I look sickly. My skin paler, my cheeks sunken in, and my under eyes are a deep purple. I see the pile of un-eaten toast next to my bed and realize I should've eaten something. This last week has been such a blur. I haven't been eating as much as I thought I have. Deme finishes my hair, and we make our way downstairs together. I pick an apple out of the fruit bowl and begin to cut it into little slices when I hear footsteps behind me.

"Thank you for coming with us." My father's voice says.

"I didn't have a choice," I tell him, putting a slice of apple into my mouth.

"There is always a choice." He says, and I choke on my apple. So that's who I learned it from. I force the apple down and turn to him.

He is dressed in a suit. The same suit that he wore to my mother's funeral. I hoped I would never see it again. Phoenix is with him, although he came in much quieter. He is dressed in a similar suit to our fathers. I didn't know he was coming with us.

Andrew's funeral is being held outside at the local cemetery. It isn't the biggest cemetery, but it is surrounded by these huge iron fences. Looking at it, you'd think they built them to keep the dead inside if a zombie apocalypse broke out, but it's probably so the wild animals don't try to dig up the bodies, which is equally disturbing. We make our way to the big white tent where the funeral will be, and I'm surprised by how many people are here. I recognize most of them from school, and it seems like our entire grade has shown up. But there are also people here in military uniforms. Andrew's dad is a Drill Instructor with the United States Marine Corps. These people in uniform are undoubtedly his Marine buddies.

I find Andrew's mom passing out programs near the back of the seating and go to her.

"Rose! I'm glad you made it." Blair pulls me into a tight hug, she sounds cheerful, but I can tell she is forcing back her tears. I don't know what to say to her, though. "I saved you a seat up front next to us. We'll talk later, honey." She says. She hands me a program, and I turn to walk to my seat when I notice Gabby. She is sitting in one of the back rows and is crying. There is no effort to hide her tears either, as people walk past her, she sobs loudly into her tissues. I'm about to keep going and avoid her when I suddenly feel guilty. It isn't her fault he is gone, it's mine.

"Hey Gabby, do you want to sit upfront with me? I think Andrew would have wanted that." I ask her when I reach where she is sitting. She looks at the person next to her, who I assume this is her mother, and they nod to each other before Gabby gets up and links her arm in mine. Although I would have preferred not to be touched by someone covered in so much mucus and tears, I don't pull away. Today is not about me. We take our seats upfront, directly in front of a large picture of Andrew.

It is one of those pictures that they take for the yearbook. You sit on a box; they tilt your head and then tilt it some more and take the photo of you sitting awkwardly in front of a green screen. I never had a good photo taken for the yearbook, but Andrew's photo is good. Although you can't see the freckles in his golden eyes, his jawline looks defined, and he comes off as more muscular than how skinny I remember him.

The music begins, and everyone takes their seats. A pastor comes out from somewhere and begins to address the crowd. He thanks the crowd for coming, tells them the family appreciates it, and begins to tell everyone Andrew's life story. The Palmers moved around a lot. Since Mr. Palmer is in the military, they were re-stationed every four years or so. Andrew was four when they moved to Paradise permanently, although his father still travels to California for work. I tune most of this speech out, I know mostly everything about Andrew. Now that I have my memories back, this speech only confirms that I do. We met when we started school, sat next to each other on the bus, and were friends ever since.

The pastor calls for anyone who wants to say anything to come forward. At first, it is silent, aside from the sounds of Blair sobbing into her purse. Andrew's dad is the first to stand. He is wearing his dress blues—a term that I've heard Andrew use when referring to the suit his father wore in his wedding photos—and begins to tell the crowd about how he wished he could have spent more time with his son. As the speeches go on, I find myself sinking further and further into my chair. I want to scream, *it was me! I killed him, I'm the reason he's dead! Only he isn't dead, just trapped in the underworld!* Instead, I look at anything but the picture of Andrew in front of me. Finally, it seems like the last person has spoken. I sigh in relief until

I find that everyone is staring at me. Of course, I would be expected to speak. I am his best friend. Gabby gives me a reassuring nudge, and I stand. I approach the pedestal and look out at everyone. Jessica is here, Joe—Demes boyfriend—is here, the whole football team. I'm not sure if I can do this. I look at Deme, who, out of everyone in the crowd, is still sitting up straight, she hasn't cried yet. It is her, who I look at when I start my speech.

"I didn't prepare a speech; I didn't even expect to say anything. But Andrew would have wanted me to." What am I doing up here? How am I going to get through this? "Some of you may know already, but my name is Rose Knight. I was Andrew's best friend. I find it difficult to pinpoint an exact moment that I want to talk about. There are so many memories that I have with him. We grew up together, did almost everything together. He loved the smell of grass in the morning, especially if it was freshly mowed. He liked listening to the airplanes overhead. His favorite color was red, not firetruck red, but more of a maroon—although he would never admit that it was really maroon." I get a few laughs from the crowd.

"He was loyal. No matter what he was going through at the time, he would always drop what he was doing to help a friend. When I lost my memory, he stood by my side through everything. When my mom died, he let me cry on his shoulder and always tried his best to make me feel better. I will never find a friend like him, and no one will ever replace him. I will forever remember him as a friend and as a brother." I look at the empty casket next to me, "Thank you, Andrew. I will never forget you. I promise."

Only a few of us stay to watch the casket get lowered into the ground. Deme holds my hand tightly, grounding me to her as if I'm going to jump into the ground with it. Gabby was too emotional to stay, so her mother took her off to the small pond nearby to calm down. Once the casket is in the ground, we drop red roses onto the top of it, and everyone begins to disperse through the crowd.

"Are you ready to go home?" Deme asks me, still clutching my hand in hers.

"Yeah, I think so," I tell her. I look around at the crowd of people. Most of the kids from school are gone now. There is most likely going to be a party tonight in Andrew's honor. It was something we always did when someone died. Honestly, it was just an excuse for them all to get drunk, and I certainly don't want to be a part of it. None of them even knew Andrew, not like I did.

I notice a woman in a black dress and matching sunhat staring at Gabby and her mother. I can't tell who she is, but for some reason, I feel the need to go to her.

"Actually, Deme, I'll meet you at the car, okay?" I tell her, she hesitantly lets go of my hand, and I walk away from her. I can feel her eyes watching me as I walk away.

"Excuse me?" I say to the woman in black as I approach her. She turns to me, and I'm forced to take a step back. There is only one person I know with a perfect hourglass figure and blonde hair that goes to her knees. Aphrodite.

"What are you doing here?" I demand, and her lips curl into a smile.

"I've never understood this tradition." She ignores my question and gestures to where the casket was lowered.

"I asked, what are you doing here?" I repeat, and she rolls her eyes at me.

"If you must know. I am here to mourn to loss of true love." She says.

"What?" I ask.

"Do I have to spell it out for you? I am the Goddess of love!" She doesn't even try to keep her voice down, "And that girl over there, crying with her mother–" she gestures to Gabby, "Has lost her soulmate." Andrew and Gabby were soulmates? I feel even worse.

"How do you know they were soulmates?" I ask her.

"You can't take my word for it? Hello! Everyone has a soulmate, even the Gods. It is my job to know who everyone's soulmate is." She explains.

"But you aren't allowed to—"

"Meddle in human affairs." She finishes, "And I don't meddle, which is why your world severely lacks in love. Thousands of people end up with the wrong person, so when someone actually finds their soulmate, I try to celebrate it as much as I can before, well before Hades forces them apart again." Aphrodite explains, and I find myself staring at Gabby. Something inside of me stirs. Jealousy? No, that never existed in my relationship with Andrew, and if they are really soulmates, then who am I to come between them?

I'm the girl who came between them. I am the one who took him away from her.

"You don't have one, you know." Aphrodite states.

"Excuse me?" I turn to her, suddenly enraged.

"A soulmate. You are the only exception. I can't tell who yours is."

"What are you talking about?" I spit.

"Zagreus and I don't like each other for a number of reasons. Most of which circle back to the fact that I have no control over him. None. I have no idea who his soulmate is. Although I have my assumptions." She looks me up and down before turning to leave.

"Wait! What are you saying?" I call out to her, but she only laughs in response before getting into a black Cadillac. I watch as the car pulls away from the cemetery.

"Rose." I turn at my name and find myself face to face with Zagreus.

END OF BOOK ONE

Acknowledgments

I have had more help on this book, than I could have ever possibly imagined. My heartfelt thanks to my family and friends, both near and far, who have cheered me on these many years as I have pursued this dream of writing novels. Your support and excitement carried me through my most challenging days.

My sister, Nikol, without you I would have given up on this crazy dream long ago. You are the reason this book exists in more ways than one. Without your love and support, none of this would have been possible. You read the whole book in less than a week and helped me mold this story into what I always dreamed it would be.

My Brother-in-law Matt, for enduring all of the questions about the Marines that stumped me. Any errors about the Military that may have ended up in my manuscript are my doing, not his.

My mother, Nisa, for always believing in me. Thank you for being so excited to hear more about this book and waiting so long to read it. None of this would have happened without your supporting soul.

My brother, Ryan, I wouldn't have had this dream of writing books if I hadn't watched you write one first. Thank you for always knowing that I could do this and inspiring my young mind.

My Father, Scott, who I credit all of my creativity to. I miss you more than anything. Thank you for always believing in me. I wish you could be here to see this all come together.

Chase, you stood by my side every step of the way. You helped me brainstorm ideas and listened patiently when I excitedly told you all about this novel. Even with all of the spoilers I've given you, you still wanted to read it. Your unconditional support has filled my heart with happiness. I will always be grateful for you.

One of my biggest champions from my very first draft was my best-friend Taylor. Thank you for taking my author photo and being a joy to be around these many years. You always knew I could do it, but I wouldn't have had nearly as much fun without you.

Shaylah, Zak, Clayton and Crystah, it was all that time we spent together at the "cabin" that really pushed me into deciding on writing a book. You all forced me out of my introverted shell and the memories you gave me will always be held in a special part of my heart.

My editor Vlad, who helped shaped this story into the best version it could be. Your kind words helped push me to release this book and to stop doubting my own abilities. Thank you from the bottom of my heart.

Rosie, you helped inspire me to write Rose and part of you will live on forever through her. Thank you.

To the musicians that unknowingly provided the soundtrack to my novel in my head.

And finally, to the readers who decide to give this book the chance. I will forever be grateful for all of you.

R.L. Nelson has been creating stories longer than she can remember.

Randee Lee was raised in the heart of Arizona, Payson. Her childhood was spent surrounded by family, animals, and books. What started as a love for storytelling, became her lifelong passion. She is happiest during winter, where you can find her in front of the fireplace, surrounded by Christmas lights, drinking hot cocoa, and cuddled up with a good book. When she isn't writing (or reading) you can find Randee painting, hiking, or playing video games in her childhood home with her two lap dogs, Sassy and Spunky.